P9-DNZ-156

Oh, she was doing it.

She was kissing him. Her mouth brushed his and a streak of heat went through her that she couldn't deny. She pulled away almost the instant their mouths touched. "I'm sorry," she said.

He turned her to face him, his hands curved around her forearms, and gripping the edge of the bar, pinning her there. "You just kissed me."

"I did," she said.

And suddenly, she found herself being hauled toward him, and he wrapped his arm around her waist, pushing her body against his. When he kissed her, he did not move away.

No. His kiss was deep, hard. Hot.

And it was Jace.

And he was kissing her. His lips were firm and expert, and then he angled his head, and she opened her mouth to him. And his tongue slid against hers. Jace's tongue.

And she was trembling. Because her fantasies had primed her for this moment over the course of years, and yet it was so much better than she had ever imagined that it could be.

* * *

One Night Rancher by Maisey Yates
is part of The Carsons of Lone Rock series.

**Select praise for *New York Times*
bestselling author Maisey Yates**

"Her characters excel at defying the norms and
providing readers with...an emotional investment."

—*RT Book Reviews* on *Claim Me, Cowboy*
(Top Pick)

"A sassy, romantic and sexy story about two
characters whose chemistry is off the charts."

—*RT Book Reviews* on *Smooth-Talking Cowboy*
(Top Pick)

"This is an exceptional example of an opposites-
attract romance with heartfelt writing and solid
character development.... This is a must-read
that will have you believing in love."

—*RT Book Reviews* on *Seduce Me, Cowboy*
(Top Pick)

"Their relationship is displayed with a quick writing
style full of double entendres, sexy sarcasm and
enough passion to melt the mountain snow!"

—*RT Book Reviews* on *Hold Me, Cowboy*
(Top Pick)

MAISEY YATES

—

ONE NIGHT RANCHER

If you purchased this book without a cover you should be aware
that this book is stolen property. It was reported as "unsold and
destroyed" to the publisher, and neither the author nor the
publisher has received any payment for this "stripped book."

Recycling programs
for this product may
not exist in your area.

ISBN-13: 978-1-335-58162-4

One Night Rancher

Copyright © 2023 by Maisey Yates

All rights reserved. No part of this book may be used or reproduced in any
manner whatsoever without written permission except in the case of brief
quotations embodied in critical articles and reviews.

This is a work of fiction. Names, characters, places and incidents
are either the product of the author's imagination or are used fictitiously.
Any resemblance to actual persons, living or dead, businesses,
companies, events or locales is entirely coincidental.

For questions and comments about the quality of this book,
please contact us at CustomerService@Harlequin.com.

Harlequin Enterprises ULC
22 Adelaide St. West, 41st Floor
Toronto, Ontario M5H 4E3, Canada
www.Harlequin.com

Printed in U.S.A.

Books by Maisey Yates

The Carsons of Lone Rock

Rancher's Forgotten Rival
Best Man Rancher
One Night Rancher

Gold Valley Vineyards

Rancher's Wild Secret
Claiming the Rancher's Heir
The Rancher's Wager
Rancher's Christmas Storm

Copper Ridge

Take Me, Cowboy
Hold Me, Cowboy
Seduce Me, Cowboy
Claim Me, Cowboy
Want Me, Cowboy
Need Me, Cowboy

For more books by Maisey Yates,
visit maiseyyates.com.

You can also find Maisey Yates on Facebook,
along with other Harlequin Desire authors,
at Facebook.com/HarlequinDesireAuthors!

To Nicole Helm, who is always here for my 11:11 texts and stories of visits I've had with birds. There is infinite value in having a friend who just gets you.

One

"You have to spend the night in the hotel if you want to buy it. Because they had too many people back out. Isn't that completely wild, Grandpa? I mean, I'm sure that it is haunted. Nothing can be around that long and not be."

Cara Summers looked up at her grandfather. He was sitting on the shelf behind the bar. In an old Jack Daniel's bottle.

Just as he had asked.

Cara had done her very best to fulfill his last wishes. Cremated and then placed on that shelf behind the bar so he could see everything.

He didn't answer her question.

At least not audibly. She didn't expect him to. Though she often felt his presence. It wasn't anything she could really describe. But she knew he was there. It was why she talked to him. Almost as easily as she had when he was here. Hell, maybe it was even easier because he didn't interrupt.

"The bar is empty, scrap. Who are you talking to?"

She knew the voice. She didn't have to turn.

Even if she didn't recognize the tone—and of course she would, after this many years of friendship. It was the way it made her feel. Because that was the thing. Jace Carson was one of six brothers. They all sounded relatively similar. Deep, rich male voices. But not a single one of them made goose bumps break out over her arms or made a suspicious warmth spread all through her body when they spoke. No. That would be way too convenient. Kit Carson liked to flirt with her, or at least he had before he had married Shelby Sohappy. And Flint enjoyed flirting with her to rile Jace up. But she knew that none of it was serious. Well. She had a feeling that any number of the Carson brothers would've happily had a dalliance with her if she was of a mind. They weren't exactly known for their discernment when it came to women. Every one of them except for Jace. Oh, Jace wasn't discerning either. But Jace was...

He was not interested in her that way. And just the mere suggestion of it made him growl.

They were friends. Best friends. Had been since middle school. It was a funny friendship. He was protective of her. And sometimes a little bit paternalistic. Or brotherly. But that was the thing. He saw her as a younger sister. The younger sister he no longer had, she knew.

And in some ways, she was an emotional surrogate for what he had lost when he had lost Sophia. She knew that. She'd always known it.

Every so often these days it made her feel bristly and annoyed.

Because the problem with Jace was that she wanted him.

And he didn't want her.

"Just telling Grandpa about my next move."

"Right," he said looking around the bar. "Is he here now?"

"He's always here," she said, gesturing to the makeshift urn.

"Cara…"

"I know you don't believe in any of this. But I do. I believe that I can talk to him. And that he hears me."

"I'm sure that's comforting."

"I think that sounds more condescending and less accepting than you think."

"I don't mean to be condescending. But I don't really mean to be accepting either. Just… I can understand why you need to think it, I guess."

That was Jace. He just didn't have a fantastical bone in his body.

He himself was a wonder. A masculine wonder. Over six foot but with broad shoulders, a well-muscled chest and not a spare ounce of fat over his six-pack abs.

He had a square jaw and compelling mouth with the thin white scar that ran through his upper lip. His nose was straight, his eyes the color of denim. Each Carson brother was sort of the same man in a different font, a remix of very similar and very attractive features.

It seemed kind of unfair that all six of them were just there. Exposing the female populace to their overwhelming male beauty. But there they were.

The really unfair thing was that none of their particular beauty called to her the way that Jace's did.

When she had been a kid, the first time she'd met him, it was like the hollow space had opened up inside of her chest, just to make room for the sheer enormity of the feelings that he created within her.

She could still remember that moment.

She'd been so angry. And so hurt. Wearing one of her oversize T-shirts to school, her grandfather's wristwatch, a pair of secondhand sneakers and jeans with holes in the knees. She had a brand-new pink binder that her grandfather had gotten her, and she knew that it had been a big deal. There were so many years where the bar that her grandpa owned—The Thirsty Mule—barely made ends meet, particularly back then. The downtown of Lone Rock had been functionally dead in the early 2000s. All the way up until the 2010s, and there just hadn't been a whole lot of money to go around.

Most of the shops back then had signs in the window that they were for sale or rent, while they sat empty.

Not only that, her grandpa just hadn't known what to do with a young granddaughter that he had taken in a few years earlier.

He loved her. Fiercely. But he had all sons, and his wife was long gone. And the gesture of buying her the pink Trapper Keeper that she had wanted so much had been... It had meant the world to her.

But there was a group of girls at the school who lived to terrorize her. For being tall and skinny and flat chested. For not being cool at all. For the fact that half of her clothes were men's, and certainly weren't in fashion. For her long blond hair, her freckles, her horse teeth...

She was occasionally amused by those memories. Because suddenly at age sixteen her boobs had come in, and when they had come in, it had been a real boon. She was stacked now, thank you very much. And it turned her a pretty impressive amount in tips on a nightly basis at the bar.

Whatever.

She thought maybe she should feel a little bit guilty that sometimes she wore a low-cut top to collect a bit more cash. But then she thought of the girl that she had been in seventh grade. The one who'd had *president of the itty-bitty titty committee* written on the outside of her locker door. And then she pulled the tank top lower and leaned toward the patron with a big smile. Everybody had their childhood trauma.

But, her breast boon notwithstanding, she could clearly remember when that same group of girls had taken that light Trapper Keeper with its beautiful white butterflies and tossed it into the dirt.

And one of the boys on the football team had held her back while they'd made sure that it was irreparably torn and stained.

She hadn't let them see her cry. No, she turned around and punched the boy right in his face. And then she got sent to the principal's office. For fighting.

"What was I supposed to do? He was holding on to me."

"You're supposed to go and get a teacher," the principal had said, maddeningly calm.

"Why wasn't a teacher there to help?"

"They can't be everywhere at once. You can't retaliate. You have to get help."

She had decided that was bullshit. Then and there. She had burned with anger.

And in fact, had said as much to the principal. *"That's bullshit."*

"Young lady, we can't tolerate that language."

And that was how she had found herself suspended, because she had thrown even more language in the principal's direction. And the funny thing was, she had just been channeling her grandpa and the way he talked on any given Sunday.

But then, that was the root of the problem. Everything about her was wrong. Wrong on some level. She said the wrong words, and more, the wrong things. She didn't know how to be a girl. Whatever that meant. Except that she knew that she wasn't even in the same species as those other girls. And not just because she wasn't a bitch. They had really been bitches. They were *still* bitches.

But she had ended up crying down by the river behind the school. Not sure how she was going to go home and tell her grandfather that she was suspended for a week.

And she was trying to wash the dirt off the binder, scrubbing at it in the water, trying to find a way out of her misery.

And that was when he'd appeared.

He'd been in eighth grade. Tall and lanky at the time, with shaggy blond hair. His family had only come to town a couple of years before, and any other family would have still been considered new. But while the Carsons hadn't lived in Lone Rock for a few years, they owned land there and were part of the original founding families, so they were considered foundational, not new.

"Hey," he said. "What's the matter?"

"Nothing," she said. "Well. Everything. First of all, middle school is bullshit."

"Right," he said. "No argument from me. Why are you crying?"

"I got suspended. Because these girls ruined my binder. And this boy was holding on to me so that I couldn't stop them. So I punched him in the face."

"Good," he said, nodding decisively.

"Then I told the principal that I thought middle school was bullshit."

"And that's why you're suspended?"

"Yes."

"It all sounds reasonable to me. Not the suspension. Everything you did. The question is, why didn't it seem reasonable to the principal?"

"I can't answer that."

"I'm Jace Carson. What's your name?"

And she suddenly felt shy and self-conscious. Because he was an older boy. And he was just so... Cute. And older boys, or boys her age, or really any boys, never talked to her.

"I'm Cara Summers. But I warn you. I'm not cool. And they call me horse teeth. And if you talk to me, they probably won't think you're cool either."

"Seventh graders? I'm fine with that."

He had walked her home. He had helped her explain the situation to her grandpa. And then he had helped with some chores around the property.

He told her a couple days later, after he came by to visit and finish some of the work, she reminded him of his sister.

He hadn't explained any of that then.

But later, about six months into their friendship, he told her that he had a sister who would be her age now. One who had died when she was a little girl. "You remind me of her. Makes me want to look out for you. The way that I looked out for her."

And that was it. They had really been best friends ever since then. Through a whole lot of things.

She'd admired him, for years. Just looked up to him like he was a god.

And she felt weird and possessive, and hadn't particularly liked it when he had girlfriends.

Not that he ever had them for all that long.

And she knew that when he was out riding in the rodeo he did a lot of casual hooking up. But she just did her best not to think about that.

It wasn't until one night at the bar, when she had been back there helping her grandpa, that she had really watched him putting the moves on a woman. He had his hand on her hip, and then he'd let it drift slowly up to her waist, and Cara had felt a physical, visceral response to it.

And that was when she'd realized.

It was when she'd realized that she wasn't just possessive. She didn't just admire him.

She was attracted to him.

She wanted him to touch her like that.

And she thought about saying something. About asking him if he would be her… It was so embarrassing. If he would be her first. Because she trusted Jace, so, it seemed like a pretty reasonable idea.

But then her grandpa had died. And that had been one of the single most devastating, destabilizing things that had ever happened. And in the four years since, she had done her level best to build herself back up. To take the bar and build it up. And handily, Lone Rock was having a bit of a boom, a resurgence. People were enjoying traveling locally, taking road trips, spending time in small towns.

There were all these posts that went up on the internet. These most charming small town posts, and Lone Rock was almost always there, as an 1800s gold rush town that still had original Western facades on a bunch of the buildings. With outlaw lore deeply embedded into the dirt all around, it was an attractive place for people to come and visit. Which was why she was now ready to invest in the hotel property. She wanted to reopen it. She wanted to get it online. It was haunted, that was the thing. And ghost stays were incredibly popular.

It was just that there had been three buyers that had backed out, and now the seller—who didn't live in Lone Rock—was demanding that potential buyers spend at least one night there to prove that they could handle it. To prove that they knew what they were getting into.

She wasn't afraid. In fact, she loved that stuff. It was just the idea of spending the night there alone...

It didn't really appeal.

But that was future Cara's problem. Right now, she had a bar to run, and Jace was here.

"What brings you in?" she asked.

"Beer. And a burger. I figured I would try to miss the evening rush. It's too hard to talk to you when you've got all those bros crowded around the bar drooling on you."

She rolled her eyes. It was the funny thing about her relationship with Jace. It wasn't like they didn't acknowledge those kinds of things. He talked about men panting after her all the time and was often growling at his brothers when they made commentary that was specifically designed to rile him up.

And she often talked about the way women acted like fools around him.

But they didn't make it personal. It wasn't about what he thought about her. But what other men thought.

And of course she never shared any actual details about her love life.

Well. Probably because she didn't have one.

That was irrelevant.

"Nobody drools," she said. "And even if they did, I don't mind if they leave tips."

"Yeah. Well, the place has become awfully popular."

"It's definitely different than it used to be."

"Too bad Mitch never got to see it."

"Of course he sees it," she said. "Like I said. He's here all the time."

"So you're telling me that his spirit lives on, and he's still hanging out in the shitty bar?"

"That's back to what I'm telling you. Anyway, I was just telling him about the hotel."

"You still fixating on that?"

"Yes. I'm going to until I get to buy it. There's just one weird little hoop to jump through. There were a couple of other offers in, but they fell through, because when they were looking around the place, there was some stuff that was… A little disconcerting. So now the owner is demanding that somebody spend the night there before they put in an offer. So… I'm gonna spend the night."

"You're gonna spend the night in the hotel? Why?"

"Because it's haunted. That's what I mean, people keep backing out because there's all this haunting stuff. I guess he's come close to selling it twice, and they were about to sign the papers when something spooky happened. So…"

"So you have to spend the night in the place to prove that you're not going to back out on the sale?"

"Yep."

"That's the dumbest thing I've ever heard. Why is he letting people with overactive imaginations cause so much grief? And why give any credence to it?"

"It works in my favor—it gave me enough time to get all my finances together. Anyway, I *want* it to be haunted," she said. "I can get it on the national list of most haunted places in the United States. People come from all over to stay in haunted hotels. It's something they're fascinated by."

"I don't want to stay in a haunted hotel. Because that's how I know the owner is a pancake short of a full stack."

"So you think I am not playing with a full deck?"

"I think that you are a bull short of a herd."

"Rude."

He shrugged. "Sorry if you don't like it."

"I don't think you are. I think you're always far too happy to give out your opinion."

"Oh well. You keep me around. Did you put my order in with the kitchen?"

She groused, but punched his burger order in at the register, then went over to the tap to pull a draft beer for him. She knew what he liked. She didn't have to ask. She had it in the glass, and he took a seat at the bar. There were only three other patrons inside, and they were in the corner next to the jukebox, not listening to anything that was happening over at the bar, from her conversation with Jace to her earlier conversation with her grandpa.

"It would be nice not have to be at the bar all day every day. If I make some money with the hotel, I can hire more people."

"Except, it's a huge additional expense."

"I know that. I've saved up for it. I can afford it.

Especially if I can get it to a certain capacity during the high tourist times. But there's just not much in the way of lodging around here. Yeah, there's vacation rentals, but the only other hotels are thirty to forty minutes away. Hotel right downtown would really be something."

"You know, if you need money…"

"I'm not taking your money. I've basically been taking your charity since eighth grade, and I have no interest in continuing to do it," Cara said.

"It's not charity. It's friendship. Anyway. When are you fixing to spend the night in the hotel?"

"Tomorrow night. I'd… I don't know. There's no real furnishings in there. It's going to be a little bit… Bracing." She wrinkled her nose.

"I don't really like the idea of you staying in a big empty insecure place by yourself. Especially not when some people might know that you're staying there," Jace said.

"I stay at the place I *live* by myself all the time."

"I don't know. This just feels different to me. I'm not comfortable with it. I should stay there with you."

"That's fine," she said, ignoring the slight jumping in her stomach when he offered that.

She had spent the night with Jace any number of times. Mostly camping. But, what would this be if not camping? They would end up bringing sleeping bags and probably a space heater.

It would just be like all the things they'd done when they were kids.

"Yeah, all right. That sounds good. In fact, now the burger's on the house."

"Why? You don't have to pay me to stay with you. I want to keep you safe."

"You get a free burger because you're submitting yourself to going on a ghost journey with me. And I know how much you hate that stuff."

"Please don't tell me you actually think that it's haunted."

"I think it might be. It stands to reason. It's historic. There were so many gunfights in this town back in the day…"

"Why are you talking to me about ghosts like there's anything logical about them? Come on. It's ridiculous, Cara, and I think on some level you must know that."

"I do not. It is as reasonable and logical as anything else in this world, Jace. And you know what, you'll see. I think that we will have a haunting."

"I don't think so."

"If we don't, it'll be because he's scared away by all your skeptic energy."

"Well isn't that convenient. An even better reason for you to have me out. Because if you don't see a ghost, you can blame me."

"Don't be silly, Jace. I always blame you."

Two

"She thinks it's haunted," Jace said, looking at his brothers that night as they sat around the table outside at the Carson family ranch.

Their mom had ordered a big spread from the barbecue place on the outskirts of town, and they were all enjoying a meal together. Well, everybody except Buck, who hadn't been home in nearly a decade. But the rest of them were there, including Chance and Kit and their wives. Callie wasn't there, because she lived in Gold Valley with her husband, but that was a different sort of absence than Buck's.

Callie wasn't home because she had a life. A happy, functional life. Buck wasn't home because he was a mess.

And what they had around the table was like a strange, evenly divided set of teams. Kit and Chance, settled with their wives, done with the rodeo. Flint and Boone, single, happy about it and definitely not done punishing their bodies on the circuit.

They were all very certain in those things.

And for some reason, more and more, Jace wasn't.

He had never been one to wallow in uncertainty. Or even entertain it. You couldn't do that as a bull rider. You needed a clear eye, a firm grip and some big balls. And he had all three, thanks. It wasn't uncertainty, more a feeling of the world shifting, and it being harder to plant one foot in Lone Rock and one in the rodeo.

A sense that he was going to have to pick.

Maybe it had to do with Cara buying the hotel. Watching her commit to this life so deeply.

"And you're spending the night with her?" Boone asked, a sly smile curving his lips.

"I spend the night with Cara all the time."

He ignored the looks that he got from all of his brothers. And he ignored the fact that it was a lie. He and Cara had camped occasionally together when they were kids and hadn't really done that as adults, but, whatever.

She was his friend.

And really, more like a sister.

He could still remember the first time he'd ever met her. Crying but angry. So angry. And he had just loved that spirit. That great fighting spirit that she had.

It had drawn him to her right away.

And it had just made him want to… Protect her. Protect her in a way that he had never been able to protect Sophia…

"Oh yeah. Adult sleepovers?" That question came from Kit, who got an elbow in the chest from his wife.

"No," he said. "Because we're friends. And unlike you assholes, I actually don't see it as a conflicting thing to have a platonic friendship with a woman. Because I see her as a whole human being and not a sex object." His sisters-in-law, Juniper and Shelby looked at each other, and then they applauded.

"Thank you," he said to them.

"Our husbands are animals," said Shelby.

"And jackasses," said Juniper.

"I know that," said Jace. "I really don't know how the two of you put up with them."

"They're hot," said Shelby.

"Well," said Jace, frowning. "That kind of bums me out. Next time, don't take it there."

"Sorry," said Shelby, grinning.

"The point of the story," said Jace, "is that she thinks the place is haunted."

"And you don't?" Flint asked.

"I don't believe in that shit. You can't tell me that… I mean, come on."

"There's a lot of things in the world that can't be

explained," said Kit. "I would never presume to know whether or not there were ghosts."

"I would," said Jace. "I presume it. You can't see it, you can't measure it, you can't prove it."

"You can't disprove it," Boone pointed out.

"Oh, shut the hell up, Boone," said Jace. "That's not a valid point and you know that."

"Seems valid enough to me."

"I don't see why you're all so invested in harassing me about Cara, anyway. She's been my best friend since middle school."

"It's because it makes you mad," said Boone. "It's that simple. And you fall for it every time, little brother. It's one of my favorite things about you."

He scowled. It really was a bitch being the youngest out of these jackasses. Well, the youngest except for Callie.

Callie had come much later, her parents hoping for another girl after the loss of Sophia.

But he was the youngest boy, and often the subject of quite a bit of harassment. Which was fine. It was just that he wished he wasn't such a chronic youngest that he fell for it.

But maybe that was one reason that Cara had felt so important to him when they had first met.

She filled the gap in the family. A gap in his life.

He had that other person, right there. He loved his sister Callie. But she was a *baby* sister.

Sophia had been close in age, and Cara was more like that.

He had just… He had just missed Sophie so damn much. That dynamic they had. Then he'd met Cara.

"Well, alternatively, you could all grow up."

Boone grinned. A big, broad smile that made Jace want to punch him. "I know you are but what am I?"

So he did punch him. Just in the shoulder.

"You're the worst."

"I know," said Boone.

And the thing was, maybe nobody would ever understand his relationship with Cara. He needed it. She was maybe the single most important person in his life, as much as he loved his family.

She had needed him, and that mattered to him.

Because the rest of his family… It wasn't the same. His parents needed Callie in a particular kind of way, because she had healed them.

They had needed Buck, who would then abandon them. And their older sons had taken on a lot of the burden.

Their father was so into the rodeo, and they all rode in the rodeo. It was just there was an excess of them.

So one of them wasn't particularly more important than the other in all of that.

But as far as Cara went? She needed him.

He looked out across the table, at the barn, and saw a bright white butterfly land on the bright red wood.

It fluttered its wings for a second before it lifted off again and continued on his way. That moment sort of reset his thoughts, cleared them out.

He wanted to help her and he… Dammit, he worried about her making a big business move like this without him around. There would be repairs needing done, and systems to set up…

She needed him, and he guessed on some level he needed to be needed. Which was why he was submitting himself to the ridiculous ghost thing—even though all of that made him irrationally angry—and why he wasn't going to let his brothers make him too angry with all their nonsense.

As far as they went, their nonsense didn't matter.

What mattered was Cara.

And making sure she was taken care of. So that was exactly what he would do.

The old hotel building was beautiful. It was at the very end of Main Street. A three-story building with balconies and wooden porch rails. Old Western lettering that said Lone Rock Hotel. She could imagine it repainted. The gold around the border of the letters brightened.

She could imagine it lit up bright in the night. Filled with guests.

It would be like…

Almost like a family.

She shook that intrusive thought off. She hadn't expected it. And it wasn't particularly welcome.

Then she heard the sound of an old truck pulling up to the place and she turned and saw Jace.

"Hi," she said, even though he was still in the truck. She waved, so that he knew that she had greeted him.

She immediately felt kind of silly.

She cleared her throat and tucked her hair behind her ear.

She still felt like a lanky, gangly teenage girl around Jace sometimes. And that was silly. But then... The whole thing with him was often silly. She was comfortable with him. More comfortable than any other living human being. But at the same time, there were moments of intense awkwardness. Moments where she was so deeply aware of what she felt.

And in those moments she became unbearably self-conscious. In a way she just... Never was around other men. She thought it was funny that she tended to make them self-conscious. She wasn't overly concerned with her appearance, and she didn't spend a ton of time on it. But, she liked to put on a little bit of makeup and enjoyed a little bit of cowgirl bling. Studded belts and tank tops with a little bit of rhinestone energy.

She liked the attention that got her.

She never worried one way or another if random

men thought she was pretty. If they did, great. If not, she didn't care.

And yet, all that insecurity came back to her sometimes when she stood there looking at Jace. And she could never really quite reconcile all of those things. The fact that in general she was more confident than she had ever been and the fact that she was often the most comfortable around him. Then also the least.

He got out of the truck, and she shoved all of those things off to the side.

"I hope you brought a sleeping bag," she said.

"Yeah I did," he said.

"I brought a space heater too," she responded. "You know ghosts can really bring down the temperature."

She watched his facial expression as he made the clear, deliberate decision to ignore her ghost comment. "Are we meeting anybody?"

"Other than ghosts?"

"Cara."

She smiled. "No. We got sent a code to open up a lockbox on the back door. So let's go hunting for it."

She went around back and she could hear his footsteps as he followed her.

She felt unbearably self-conscious of the fact that he might be watching her.

She banished that. It was Jace. They were friends. Maybe it was the strangeness of spending the night with him, but it wasn't like they had never done that before. Of course they had.

It had just been a long time, because they were grown-ass people, and they didn't tend to have sleepovers anymore. Or camping trips.

But they had. This was hardly singular.

"How did the rest of the night go last night?" he asked.

"Just fine. Like always. I know it's a shock to you, Jace, but my world turns just fine when you aren't there."

He looked at her. And it was far too clear a look.

For some reason, her stomach went tight, and she had the vague impression that maybe he could see into what had happened last night after she had gone home. No. She refused to think that. She refused to even entertain that thought. Because, if at three in the morning she had finally stumbled home and gotten into the shower, and if, when she had started to run her hands over her body as the water had cascaded over her curves, she had had a few moments where she had let herself imagine that they were Jace's hands skimming over her skin, and then maybe she had some trouble falling asleep, and she had taken those erotic thoughts to her bed with her and let them carry her off to a natural conclusion...

She really did try not to think of him that way. Yeah, it was one thing to think that he was hot; it was quite another to have actual, full-blown sexual fantasies about him, which just felt intrusive and wrong, and she always felt quite guilty after.

And she only ever did it on nights when she was really exhausted, and good sense had deserted her and…

Whatever… She supposed that she could justify that all she wanted, and the end result would still be the same. It was sort of shitty to think about your best friend like that.

And here she was, thinking about her best friend like that. Again. While he was standing right there. She cleared her throat and aggressively undid the padlock that contained the key, typing the code in with a lot more force than was strictly necessary. And then she pushed the door open and exhaled.

It was beautiful in here. She had come inside one time when she was a kid, and her grandfather had been looking at the property. It had been a pipe dream to buy it then. There had been absolutely no way. There wasn't enough tourism in town to make it worth it, and they had been financially strapped as it was.

But it had been his dream. And ever since then, it had been hers. Other than the one time they had gone inside to look at the place, she had only ever seen it from the outside looking in, and in pictures. But even now, dusty and in a bit of disrepair, it was the most beautiful place she had ever seen.

The floors were real wood, the drapes might be

full of dust and mites and God knew what else, but they were beautiful.

They would just need some cleaning.

A deep rich red, with velvet damask. The wallpaper was lovely, but would definitely need to be replaced with something authentic. It was too water-stained to be restored, she had a feeling, and anyway, it would be less expensive to simply replace it all. But the original front desk was still there, a beautiful oak that needed to be oiled—she knew all about that, because the original bar from the 1800s was still in The Thirsty Mule, and she had ample experience at taking care of it.

There was a big crystal chandelier that hung in the center of the room, and it was the thing that gave her the biggest thrill.

The entire hotel had been outfitted with electricity and indoor plumbing by the 1920s, and it was currently such a glorious mix of all the errors that had come after and the original foundation. She loved each and every layer of history.

Enough that for a moment, it had knocked her out of her Jace haze. But only for a moment.

She turned and realized that he hadn't followed her inside. And then a moment later, there he was, holding both sleeping bags, the space heater and the bag of groceries that she had brought, so that they would be able to eat something tonight.

"I like it," he said, looking inside. "Slumber party snacks."

They weren't just snacks—she had a whole charcuterie situation in there, but she couldn't find any wit rolling around in her head right now.

For some reason the words *slumber party* made her fidgety.

"You know me. I don't like to be hungry."

"Who does?"

"Well, no one I assume, but not everybody will launch a feudal war over hunger pangs. But you know I will."

"That is true."

"Anyway. This is it. Isn't it great?"

"It is a lot of space. Just this room is a lot of space. Empty space."

"I'm not destitute, Jace. I pretty obsessively squirrel money away, actually. Anyway, Grandpa had a life insurance policy, and I've got that socked away in savings too. I've been living with my belt tightened so that I can get this place. But I have it all planned."

"Yeah, and you're secretive too."

"I haven't talked to you about it because I knew that you would be… This," she said, gesturing toward him.

And then he did something that shocked her. He reached out, wrapped his hand around her wrist and made that same gesture but practically up against his chest, all over again. "What is… All this?"

The way that his calloused fingers felt against her wrists sucked all the air out of her body. She felt like she was gasping. She felt like she was losing her mind. And she couldn't remember what she had been about to say. Because he had touched her, and she hadn't been expecting it. It wasn't that they didn't touch. They did, casually enough on occasion. But there was usually a flow to it, or something that felt slightly mutual. This was combined with her fantasies last night, and the fact that they were in the hotel now...

"You're a skeptic," she said quickly, suddenly finding the words and retrieving them from deep inside of her brain. "About everything. And I needed to be able to dream about this. If I wanted skepticism, I would ask for skepticism. But I don't want skepticism. I wanted to be able to believe that something magical could happen. That I could fulfill this long-held wish that my grandfather had... And you know what, I needed to be able to believe wholly in it and in myself in order to make it happen."

"You are perilously close to sounding like one of those self-help gurus that I hate. You were practical. You worked hard. It's hardly manifesting."

"You know what, I don't see what harm manifesting does?" She was getting irritated at him, and that felt welcome. Necessary even. "You're so skeptical about everything—this is my point. There is no way that thinking negative thoughts is actually better than thinking positive ones. And I didn't need any doubt to creep in. Yes, I did have to do the work, and I acknowledged that. But I also needed to believe in order to stay motivated to do it. And you…" She decided that since he had touched her, touching him was fair game. She put her fingertips on his chest and gave him a slight shove. "You are nothing more than a Debbie Downer."

Her fingertips felt like they were burning from where they had made contact with his well-muscled chest, and she realized that it was something that had definitely punished her more than it punished him.

She folded her fingers in and rubbed them against her palm. It wasn't really a punishment, if she were honest. Touching him felt good. It was just that it led to all sorts of other thoughts that didn't have a place to go, and that was what made it all feel like torture. That was the problem.

"Right. Well. I'm sorry that you feel that way. I would've supported you, though. I do support you. And if I try to provide a…counterweight to your buoyancy, it's only because everybody needs a ballast, right?"

"I guess," she said. "I get it. I do. But the thing is, you treat me like I'm a kid. We are like a year and a half apart, Jace. There is no call to treat me like that."

"Yeah, there is," he said, his voice suddenly going gruff. "Where should I put the stuff?"

She knew what he was thinking. She knew what

he was going to say. She wasn't going to give him a chance to say it. "Well, I don't know. We have to find a bedroom. We might as well find the best one." They started to walk up the stairs. One of them creaked, but it wasn't so bad.

The carpet on the stairs was somewhat thread-bare, and she wondered if it would just be the better part of valor to get rid of all of it and reveal the honey oak beneath.

But there would be a lot of expense involved in refurbishing the place. Still, it would be worth it. And she could afford it. Really, for the first time in her life, she could afford a dream, and it was brilliant and amazing.

She was not a kid.

And she was definitely not Jace's baby sister. No matter how he acted.

The hallway was long, with numbered doors facing opposite each other. Ten in total. "All right. Let's see what we have."

The first room was entirely barren, with lace curtains that barely covered the window, and she decided that unless they had to, that wasn't going to be the room.

The next room was filled with nightstands and wardrobes and other miscellaneous furniture—a dining table and some chairs, all stacked up and filled from back to front. "Well, I guess it's good to know there's some furniture left in here. Some of it is probably salvageable. Or at least, we can use the wood for something. There's probably some local artisans that could make something great with it."

"Yeah," he said.

And she could tell that he was biting his tongue. Damn him.

He was trying—that wasn't fair.

"Let's go, so that you don't pull a muscle," she said, carrying on down the hall and opening two more doors, before deciding to open another.

And in that room, there was a bed.

A big bed that was likely full of dust and had a rich brocade bedspread on it. There were canopy curtains and matching velvet curtains over the window. It was set as if it was exactly prepared for guests. A nightstand, wardrobe, a small vanity with a bowl and a picture, which she knew would have been used as a washbasin.

"Well, here we go," she said.

"Look," he said. "I don't even believe in this haunting business, and even I know that if one of the rooms is going to have a ghost in it, it's going to be this one."

"But you don't believe in ghosts," she said. "And I want to see one, so that declaration is hardly a deterrent." She grabbed a sleeping bag out of his hand and looked around the room. "I hope you don't have allergies."

"No. Thankfully. Otherwise living on a ranch would be rough. I can deal with a little bit of dust."

"You can sleep in the bed if you want," she said, grinning at him.

"Yeah. I'll skip it."

Then suddenly, it was way too easy to imagine the two of them in a bed, and she wondered if she had miscalculated by choosing this room.

It was one thing to think about sleeping on the floor with sleeping bags—which they were still going to do—it was just that the fact that they were in a room with a big bed…

She was starting to feel a little bit sweaty. She was starting to feel a little bit shaky. Jittery. And she just didn't have the presence of mind to figure out how to not feel that way.

It's Jace.

This was the problem. It wasn't like this all the time. It was just like this sometimes, and usually for set periods of time. Like, something would happen, there would be a touch, a little bit of something that felt out of the ordinary that brushed up against her hormones, and then she would have a fantasy about him, and then things would feel awkward, but then they didn't usually spend the night in the same bedroom.

"Okay," she said, desperate for a reprieve. "You lay out the sleeping bags and get the space heater going, I'm going to go downstairs and see what I can find in the way of utensils and get some snacks prepared. And, I also brought a bunch of downloaded movies."

"Awesome. See, we don't need ghosts for entertainment. We can entertain ourselves."

Three

He stood there in the middle of the room, completely motionless for a good thirty seconds after Cara left. He could not quite figure out why there was something about his own words that hit him wrong. They could *entertain themselves*.

He also couldn't figure out why his chest still felt electrified where she had put her fingertips.

Things were a little bit weird. And he wasn't quite sure what to make of that. But he did as he was asked. He laid out the sleeping bags at the foot of the bed, then plugged in the space heater between them.

This kind of amused him. It was a little bit like a campfire.

He looked over at the bed. And he ignored the rising tension in his gut. There was no reason to be tense. His idiot brothers had gotten in his head was the thing. They specialized in that. That was what older brothers did, after all, but what they did not do was understand that Cara was a sacred object.

And Jace was not a man who fucked around with the divine.

No. He knew that he had no call ever taking her out of the category that he'd put her in all those years ago. His best friend. And the woman he wanted to protect more than anything in the whole world.

She'd had it so hard, and he just wanted to shield her from ever having another hard thing happen to her.

She wasn't a woman to him. Not really. She never had been.

Yeah. There had been the unfortunate moment in high school when she… Filled out a little bit and he'd been seventeen—nearly eighteen—and not as experienced as he was now, and it had been a little bit difficult to keep from marveling at the changes that had occurred. But that was teenage boy shit. Dumb shit.

He was a grown man.

He had been riding out on the rodeo circuit since then, and he had a hell of an education in the female form during those years.

He'd also learned a lot about himself.

There was something about having the miraculous beaten out of you at an early age that made it impossible to believe in lasting love and connections. Well, it did him.

His parents had clung together after Sophie had died. They'd had Callie. They'd kept on hoping. He supposed.

Callie, well, she hadn't been alive when Sophia had died, so while she knew, she didn't really know.

Chance and Kit, their love stories were gritty. More than they were miraculous, he supposed. They had both fallen for incredibly tough women, women who took every opportunity to take them to task when they needed it, and Jace found it amusing as hell.

He was happy that they could do that thing.

But then there was Buck, who had left town under a cloud when he was still in his early twenties. Buck, who clearly couldn't find anything miraculous to hold on to.

And Flint and Boone were as noncommittal as he was in the relationship department. Meaning, they didn't have them. Flint had quite famously broken up with the woman who'd gone on to be a famous country singer. And the song that she'd written about him—when it had hit the airwaves a couple of months ago it had caused a slight explosion.

Granted, she didn't use his name, but everybody knew it was about him. Everybody.

People around Lone Rock were too smart to mention it. But… Yeah, occasionally he and Boone would trawl the online forums looking for things to interrogate their brother about.

"Where is the scarf, Flint?"

"Yeah. Where is it?"

"I don't know what the hell you're talking about," he would growl.

"She claims you kept her scarf."

"Fuck you."

"That reminds me, there was a key chain..."

"There is no key chain," said Flint. *"It's not about me."*

Point being, he was the only one of them that had tried a relationship, and it hadn't gone well. Boone sure as hell wasn't stupid enough to even try.

He just didn't have it in him. He thought you had to be some kind of crazy to invest in a relationship like that. You had to be some kind of starry-eyed, and a hell of a lot of things he just wasn't.

He would never drag a woman through that.

He had never wanted to. He had his family, he had Cara, and that was enough.

A moment later, she returned. "Well, I managed to get this all set up." She had a tray of meat and cheese, and two wineglasses, plus a bottle of...

"Rosé?"

"You got a problem with that?"

"A prissy meat and cheese tray and a bottle of girls' night out wine?"

She stared at him blandly. "Not when there's no one else here."

She sniffed as she settled onto her sleeping bag

and set the tray out in front of her. "Your toxic masculinity is strangling you to death."

"No." He settled down on his own sleeping bag and reached out and took a wedge of cheese. "It would be if I refused to partake. But here in the sacred space…"

"You're an idiot," she said.

"Yeah. Probably."

"Are you going back out to the rodeo?"

He had been avoiding that direct question. Not even his brothers had asked. Boone and Flint were still at it, but Buck had left a long time ago, with Kit and Chance retiring recently.

Jace was younger than Boone and Flint, but he knew he was getting to about the age where you had to start considering how many permanent injuries you wanted to walk around with for the rest of your life all for the sake of chasing continued glory.

He liked a little glory, it was true, but he also valued the fact that he didn't walk with a limp, and the longer you stayed in the game the less likely that was to continue to be a thing.

Their father was on the verge of retirement, and he didn't know that any of them were chomping at the bit to become the next Rodeo Commissioner. Or maybe they were; they hadn't really talked about it. Jace wasn't, that was all he knew. The family was more and more settled in Lone Rock. And maybe that wasn't such a bad thing.

"Don't know," he said.

"You really don't know?"

"I really don't."

"That doesn't seem like you."

"Maybe not," he said, shoving some of his discomfort aside. "I don't know. Stuff is changing. It kind of started with Callie getting married a couple years ago, and now... I don't know. The family's more settled here. For a long time it seemed like my dad was just running. Running from everything. Running from his grief and all of that... But they've expanded the ranch here so much, and I think he's finally ready to quit moving around all the time. At his age, he probably should've done it a long time ago, but given that he's him... I think it might be kind of a big deal."

"That makes you think about change."

"It just makes me wonder what I'm doing. The thing is, we've all won the top tier of all the events that we've ever competed in. There's a point where the only way you can go is down. So then you ask yourself why you're doing it."

"Do you love it?"

It was a strange question. He never really thought about it. Rodeo was the family business. He knew there were spare few people for whom that was true. But since he was a kid, his father had been the Commissioner of the Pro Rodeo Association, and it had been a given that they would all grow up and compete. Callie had competed in saddle bronc events for a couple of years; she was taking a break to have a baby, which was great. That had meant a lot to her, breaking that barrier as a woman, and she had paved the way for a whole lot of other women who wanted to do the same thing.

She had a reason for being there.

Kit and Chance were top in their field. He had done bareback broncos for a number of years; he'd ridden bulls. That was all after he and his brothers had done a little bit of tie-down roping in their early years. He didn't know that he loved it so much as that he wore it comfortably like a pair of battered old jeans. And he didn't know what else fit. Ranching. They had a big family ranch.

But it was an interesting thing to grow up in a family where you didn't wonder what you would be when you grew up. There was a legacy that you inherited, and you stepped into that. But then, Cara knew about that. He doubted she owned the bar because she loved it the most. He could see that this hotel thing meant a lot to her but he had to wonder...

He gestured to the room around them.

"Is this actually something that you want, or is this just what Mitch wanted to do?"

"I actually do want it," she said. "I've loved this place since I was a kid. And yeah, some of it is that it makes me feel good to fulfill his dreams. Because he couldn't. And he was there for me. He was there for me when no one else in my family was. My dad was… I still don't know where. My mom was where she is now. Drugged out of her mind in a trailer park somewhere making bad decision after bad decision with men. And… I had Grandpa. I don't think I'm doing it just because I want them to be proud or anything like that. I'm doing it because the things that were important to him became important to me. This town became important."

"Yeah."

"I guess I have to ask you the same question. Are you in the rodeo just because it's what your dad wants you to do?"

"No. To be honest, I don't think my dad cares what we do. In fact, I think he would've been perfectly happy if we had never risked life and limb out on the circuit. He loves it, but he's realistic about the risks. Especially after that kid died a couple of years ago… He was never really the same after that. Never looked at the rodeo the same."

And that was a shame. Because the rodeo had been his dad's escape from his grief. Jace knew that, because he understood it. He moved around, and he moved around a lot. Motion kept you from thinking too deep.

But it felt like he was at a critical point. He didn't want to just keep moving. But staying felt like an invitation to settle into pain.

Of course the alternative to that was processing it, but he'd spent years avoiding that.

Years using Cara as a surrogate.

But watching her now, watching her actually take control of her life and get what she wanted shamed him a bit.

"I'm sorry. I know it was your dream…"

"It wasn't," he said. "The rodeo was easily available to us. And we had to do something. But I think it was more than that. It was easy for us to pivot into it because we knew all about it. It must be different when it's your dream. When you have to chase it. It was more like that for Callie, because Dad sure as hell didn't want her out on the horses. Drove him nuts. Still does, to be honest, but he's accepted that is something he's not gonna win with her. He's accepted that is something she's going to do, and she's a grown woman, so you can't stop her. I mean, she married Jake Daniels just to get access to her money."

He'd never anticipated the money. Didn't care about it. Didn't need it.

That shamed him a bit too.

"I never asked, do you all have trust funds like that?"

"Yeah. But we get it when we turn thirty."

"So you're getting yours soon."

He really hadn't thought much about it. He had whatever he needed. He turned quite a lot of money on the circuit; he got in a fair amount of endorsements. He had it pretty easy, honestly.

"Yeah."

"You don't know what you want to do with it?"

"I guess not."

He didn't like that. But then, thinking about the future wasn't his thing. It was that whole… Well, he guessed it was a lot like what she had accused him of. She hadn't wanted to tell him about her dreams because he had the unfortunate inclination to bring reality down on them. And as for himself… He didn't really dream.

"I don't like to think ahead. I live in the moment. I like to work. It's clarifying. In that sense, I guess I do love to ride in the rodeo. You get a surge of adrenaline not like much else. Not really like anything but sex, to be honest."

And then she blushed. All the way up her neck to the roots of her hair. Then it surprised him, because it wasn't like Cara was a prude. She worked in a bar. She heard rough talk all the time. Hell, she wandered around the place looking like *Coyote Ugly* half the time, which she could do without, and men checked her out all evening. She seemed to get a kick out of it. Because she was in control of that interaction, and could bounce their asses out of the bar if they got unruly.

He hadn't expected her to blush just because he

mentioned sex. But then he looked behind her and saw the bed, and the earlier tension returned.

"Anyway," he said, clearing his throat. "I didn't really think about what I would do with it. I didn't really think about what I would do when I was done with the rodeo. And anyway, I could coast on that for a few more years if I wanted to."

"You don't want to, though," she said, reaching out and taking a piece of cheese. She seemed to recover slightly from the earlier incident.

But he had to wonder why it had been an incident at all.

"How do you know that?"

"I know that," she said, "because it's not like you to have doubts, and you do. If you're uncertain, and you're pausing, then there's something else going on."

He didn't like that. Didn't like that shifting sand feeling underneath his feet.

It probably had to do with his brothers getting married. It was just a change.

Made him contemplate what things would look like for him, because they wouldn't look like that.

He also didn't love that she could read him so well. He needed to be able to read her. It was important. He had to protect her. Take care of her. Make sure that she was doing all right. The thing was, he had his whole big family. And since her grandfather's death, Cara had nobody. She'd always had fewer people than him. And it made him really important. It made what he did for her really important.

So yeah, he kind of prided himself on knowing what was going on with her, on keeping track of her. On making sure that everything was all right.

But the fact that she seemed to be able to read him... He wasn't sure how he felt about that.

"You know, there are some other shops on Main Street that are being sold. The businesses are still going to be there, but the buildings are up for sale..."

"Are you suggesting that I invest in real estate?"

"It's an idea."

It was. It was also... Roots. Ties. It wasn't like he was planning on leaving Little Rock. No, that didn't really factor into his plans. But he also didn't own land for a reason.

And what exactly is that reason?

He shoved that thought to the side.

"What movie are we opening with?"

"Oh," she said. "You're going to love this." She settled onto her sleeping bag, grabbing her tablet and setting it up on the floor. She rested her elbows on the sleeping bag, and her chin on her knuckles. "I thought that we needed some nostalgia."

"Oh no," he said.

"Do you remember when we skipped school and we drove down to Bend and we went to see our favorite buddy cop movie?"

"No way."

"Yes way."

"You can quote that movie in its entirety. Do you actually need to watch it again?"

"Yes I do. Because you know that if I were a lion and you were a tuna…"

"You're ridiculous," he said. But he did find it endearing. He liked that she enjoyed a raunchy comedy, just as much as he did. Though, this was not his favorite.

"Don't worry," she said. "I also have the terrible dream movie you love so much."

"Thank you."

"And you know, an array of teen movies. From *Mean Girls* to *Easy A*."

"I don't like those movies."

"I know you don't. I don't care. But we'll probably fall asleep before then, because we are not eighteen—we're old."

"Speak for yourself."

"I'm younger than you," she said.

"Yeah," he said, nudging her with his elbow.

She looked at him and wrinkled her nose, and for some reason, he found his eyes drawn to the freckles there.

They were cute. Just a little sprinkling of them that went from her cheeks over the bridge of her nose. They highlighted her green eyes somehow. Beautiful eyes. Slightly feline. She wasn't wearing makeup tonight, so her lashes were pale. Often, she wore a real dark mascara that made her eyes feel like a punch in the gut. This was more like a slow, spring sunrise. A whole lot of green and gold.

That tension had returned.

"All right. Get the movie going," he said.

"Gladly," she said, pouring a glass of wine and handing it to him, before pouring herself one. He lay back on his sleeping bag and decided to pay attention to the movie, instead of the color of her eyes.

Four

She was just so aware of him. Of every inch of him. The way that he was lying on the sleeping bag, the way that his arm shifted, the way his whole body shifted when he went to take a drink of his wine.

When he grabbed some cheese off the cheese board.

She was starting to feel light-headed, and she had a feeling she needed to go get some more food, so she wasn't off on her alcohol-to-protein ratio. But she found herself drinking a little bit faster the more her nerves flared up in her gut.

This was ridiculous.

But the problem with choosing movies that they had gone to see together in high school was that it reminded her of being in high school with him. That was when her little crush had started acting up. Oh, it wasn't when she had realized that she wanted to sleep with him—that was a more mature realization. But the butterflies over his arm brushing hers when they sat together in the movie theater… Yeah. That had been pure high school.

And she really wasn't nostalgic for it. And here she was, alone with the man in an empty house—unless there were ghosts, there could be ghosts—as an adult, having those same feelings.

It was almost funny.

It was *almost funny*, that now they were adults, absolutely alone and unsupervised, adjacent to a bed, and she was *still* in no danger of Jace Carson trying to pressure her into sex. No. She was much more likely to try to pressure him into it.

The idea made her feel lit up from the inside out. Entirely too warm. She did her level best to look back at the movie.

The next one was not her favorite. It was too mind-bending and she didn't like it. She liked things that had resolved endings, at least. She would prefer a happy ending. But the ambiguity of it all made her itchy, and she started to get restless.

"I'm going to go downstairs and get another bottle of wine," she said.

"Another bottle of wine?"

"Yes. I think that sounds like a pretty good idea, don't you?"

"Yeah. All right."

She knew it wasn't a great idea. She was already feeling a little bit wobbly and loose, and she was in such a weird precarious place with him it…

Well, she had been friends with the man for thirteen years. It wasn't like she was just suddenly going to break it.

She pondered that when she went to get the package of cupcakes, and the new bottle of wine.

Something crashed to her left and she whipped her head toward the sound and she stopped.

She waited to see if she heard another noise, waited to see if anything else shifted, but all she could hear was her own breathing. Ragged. Too fast.

"For heaven's sake," she muttered to herself.

She was such a mess.

She was being ridiculous because she was tipsy and anticipating ghosts and strung out on Jace. And maybe more wine was the wrong thing, but maybe it was the right thing because she needed to calm down. Maybe if she could loosen up, she'd get her equilibrium back.

She waited a few breaths more and didn't hear anything else, so she took the cake and wine back upstairs.

Jace was sprawled out on the sleeping bag on his back, his arm thrown over his face, his shirt lifted an inch or so, so she could see his flat, toned stomach.

Dear sweet Lord, she needed an intervention. A miracle.

Or maybe just wine.

"I'm back with more," she said, standing over him.

His mouth curved into a smile, his arm still thrown over his face, and she was so fixated on that she never saw his other hand coming.

Suddenly she found herself grabbed at the back of the knee and she shrieked, going down fast. And it was only his muscles that stopped her from crashing to the ground, as he somehow managed to guide her down to the sleeping bag slowly with *one arm*.

"Jace!" she shouted, folding down over the top of him.

He was warm under her.

And hard.

And *oh no*.

She was lying across him, folded at the waist over his chest. She scrambled hard to get off him but not before her hand made contact with his *very firm* ass.

She rolled the rest of the way off him, then scrabbled back for her wine and cake. "Why are you such a child?"

He was reclining, looking at her like…

She had to look away.

"I'm definitely not a child."

"You're immature. I heard a noise downstairs," she said, desperate to not think about the fact he was so very not a child, but clearly a man. "Maybe it was a ghost."

"Well, it wasn't. Because ghosts aren't real. But that cake looks real and I want some."

She still hadn't quite recovered from the full body Jace contact. "I don't know if you can have any because you're being mean."

"I'll take it from you."

He would too. And if there was one thing she could not handle now it was a wrestling match over cake, so she surrendered it, but she did not do it graciously.

And then she poured herself more wine.

They finished his favorite movie and then went on to hers. And she was definitely more than a little tipsy by the time they decided to put in their final comedy about a bunch of high school seniors' quest to lose their virginity.

They'd seen it a hundred times. She had no idea how they'd ever watched it before without her feeling immeasureably uncomfortable.

"Man, I don't miss high school," he said, tipping back his glass of wine. She watched his throat work, watched his Adam's apple bob up and down, and it made her feel a little bit giddy. She looked away.

"Yeah. Wasn't exactly the greatest time of my life either."

It was a lot of feeling weird and awkward. First with a flat chest, then with curves. But weird and awkward all the same.

"It's just the ridiculousness of it all. All the kids

who think they're kings and queens. Of what? The cafeteria. It's ridiculous… All the hormones. Maybe back then I should've decided what I wanted to do. But I was too busy worrying about things like that. Granted, I was a senior when I lost my virginity."

She blinked. *"No."*

Was he about to confess to her that he was an awkward, college virgin? She didn't know what to think about that.

"No. More like a junior."

In *college*? No. That was when she realized he meant…high school. When they'd been friends.

"Why didn't I know that?" she asked, her tongue feeling loose and lazy. And she was annoyed that she had asked that. But she was annoyed that he had mentioned it.

"Did you want me to tell you that I got a fake ID and went to the next town and hooked up with some woman in a bar?"

"You didn't," she said.

"No. Not kidding. That's what I did. I didn't figure that an inexperienced virgin should inflict their inexperience on another virgin, you know what I mean?"

She frowned and wrinkled her nose. "Yeah. Sure."

"I don't know. It just never seemed like the thing to me. I'm still like that. I don't like to have a fling with women too close to home."

She frowned. "Right."

They should not be having this weird, wine addled

conversation because she was already in a strange space, and now she was grumpy with it.

And they were supposed to be watching a comedy. Granted, one they had watched multiple times before, but still.

"I've never had sex with a virgin, actually," he said.

And that did something weird to her. To her body. Her soul.

And she knew, she knew that she needed to stop herself from saying something. She knew that she needed to get a grip. She knew that none of this whole conversation was about her. Or maybe it was. Maybe it was about their friendship. The fact that they were now, and had always ever been friends. So while maybe he hadn't confessed to his sexual shenanigans when they were in high school, he didn't think anything of telling her now. Which... Hurt, actually. He should be a little bit uncomfortable talking to her about sex. It should make him imagine having sex with her. She had *great* boobs.

And he was a straight man. Why wasn't he into her boobs? It wasn't fair. There were all kinds of random men at the bar who would love to see them. And Jace just seemed immune. And he was sitting there talking about sex. Like it was nothing.

"Well," she said, "I guess you're not half the stud that I thought you were," she said.

"I'm not?"

"Yeah," she said. "I would've thought that you had sex with all kinds of virgins. Corrupter of innocents and whatever."

"No," he said. "One of the few things I haven't done."

"Well," and she could hear it in her head before it came out of her mouth, and there was some reasonable rational part of her that was crouched in the corner shouting: don't say it, Cara. But that rational, reasonable part of her was drowned out by Wine Cara, who had some opinions and wanted to express them. Wine Cara was a bitch, and later, she and Wine Cara were going to have a stern conversation. But she was just on the ride right now. "If you wanted to have sex with a virgin, I can help with that."

"Excuse me? Are you offering to find me a virgin through your bar contacts?"

He didn't understand.

She could turn back now.

She didn't.

"No," she said, pushing his shoulder. "If you wanted to have sex with a virgin, just have sex with me."

Five

Jace was frozen. And for a full ten seconds you could've heard a pin drop. Except then suddenly there was a huge crash, and Cara scampered across the distance between them and pressed herself against his chest, her eyes wide. "What the hell was that?"

"I don't know," he said, and he didn't know if he was answering her question about the noise, or if it was about the fact that she had just told him she was a virgin and essentially offered to have sex with him.

His heart was thundering hard, and he told himself it was because of the crash, because it had startled him. And not because Cara was pressed up against him.

Which he told himself was because of the wine. Everything that had just happened was because of the wine. And there was no call getting all worked up about that. No call getting angry. Or reading too much into it or anything like that.

Except, they probably needed to figure out what that noise was.

"Where did it come from?" she asked.

"I don't know," he said, peeling himself away from her. But the heat from her body remained, and he felt somewhat branded by it all.

"It's probably your ghost," he said. "Didn't you want there to be a ghost?"

"I didn't want it *to scare me*," she said.

Then she looked up at him, her expression dazed. "Oh," she said.

"What?"

"I just told you I was a virgin."

"Let's put a pin in that," he said. "By which I mean let's not talk about it again."

He hadn't really meant to say the last part out loud. But he was a little bit tipsy, and even though the noise had done something to sober them up a bit, it wasn't fully complete.

"Fine then. But let's go see what it is."

She got up and started to pull on his shirt. He pushed himself up, and grabbed hold of her arm. "Whoa. Did it ever occur to you that it might actually be an intruder?"

"No," she said, her eyes wide. "I just thought it was a good old-fashioned haunting."

"What if it isn't?" he said. "That's something to

keep in mind. That's why I'm staying with you. What if one of those perverts from the bar knew that you were staying here?"

"That's creepy, Jace," she said. "If I thought that the bar patrons were like that that I wouldn't let them in."

"I don't trust anybody. Bottom line. So stay with me, and we'll go see what it is."

"I can't even tell where it's coming from." Suddenly, there was another crash, and she pressed herself against him, and he became extremely aware of the way her breasts felt against his arm. Firm and full and high. And more than a little bit enticing.

A virgin.

What the hell?

What the hell?

He did not have time to focus on that, because he needed to see what was happening down the hall. Or maybe... He stopped and listened. Maybe down the stairs.

"Did you leave anything open when you went downstairs?"

"No. I didn't open anything."

"Did you hear anything when you went down there?"

"Again," she said, "no. I didn't."

"Come on."

The sound was consistent. And raucous.

"I doubt that's a ghost," she said.

"Oh, because they aren't real?"

"No," she said. "Because it's an easy sound to follow, and anybody who had spent the night here previously could've followed it themselves. I would think that the haunting was a lot more…you know, ambiguous."

"Oh. Ambiguous haunting. As opposed to one of those big, obvious hauntings."

"Clearly," she said.

"Come on."

"Do you have like a gun or anything?"

"In a lockbox in my truck, yes. But not in the house."

"But it's where you can get to. If you need to."

"We won't need it. Whatever's going on, I'll finish it hand to hand."

He felt her relax.

"I'll take care of you," he said. "I always take care of you."

And that was when he realized he didn't want her coming toward the noise with him. "I want you to stay here," he said.

And then he turned to face her and felt like he'd been punched in the stomach. She was looking up at him, those pale lashes all spiky, her green eyes searching.

And he couldn't get their previous conversation out of his head.

Except over the top of that he felt a surge of protectiveness.

And without thinking, he reached up and touched her cheek. "Stay here."

Her eyes fluttered closed, and she swayed toward him, just slightly. And everything in him went tight. He took a step back. "I'll be right back."

He went down the stairs and toward the kitchen. The noise was definitely coming from the kitchen. From the pantry.

He heard footsteps behind him and turned sharply. "I told you to wait upstairs," he said.

"I didn't want to," she said.

"I didn't ask what you wanted, Cara. I'm protecting you."

"Well now whatever it is knows we're here," she said. "Because you're being loud."

"You're being loud," he said.

"It's coming from the pantry," she said.

"Yeah. I got that."

He reached out and opened up the pantry door, quickly. And there, inside a flour sack, he saw a big fat ring tail. There was a movement, followed by a cloud of pale white dust, and then a small masked face and two spindly claws appeared over the edge of the bag.

"What the ever-loving hell?"

"It's a raccoon," she said, sounding charmed.

"Those fucking things will eat your face off," he said.

"They're adorable," she said.

"They're menaces," he said. "All right, you little bandit, get out of there."

He was not about to call animal control over one small ring-tailed menace. Hell no. And he didn't think that was just the wine talking. He was going to be able to get it out of there.

"I hope you're happy by the way," he said. "Because I knew there was a very reasonable explanation for why people were hearing noises in the house."

"It's a raccoon," she said. "And a raccoon is not a ghost."

"That is my point."

"No," she said, shaking her head. She wobbled, and he realized that Cara was still a lot more tipsy than he was. "I mean, if it had been a raccoon the whole time, then they would've seen it. But it wasn't a raccoon the whole time. It was a ghost the rest of the time. And it's just a raccoon now."

"Whatever. I would've preferred a ghost, because then we could just have an exorcism or some shit, but it's a raccoon, and now I need to chase it out."

"I want it to be my pet."

"It can't be your pet. Don't be ridiculous." He kept watch on the creature, which was staring at him with beady eyes, and he reached into the corner of the pantry and picked up her broom. "I will use this on you," he said.

"Are you cleaning up the town, Sheriff?" Cara asked.

"You're drunk. Get out of here."

He supposed that he should feel better knowing that she was drunk. Maybe she had been teasing. About the whole virgin thing. That couldn't be true. She worked at a bar. She looked like... Like that.

And she sure as hell had to have been teasing about... Him.

"All right," he said, talking to the raccoon again as he extended the broom. "Get outta here."

It snarled and leaned forward, chewing on the bristles.

"Get out," he said, brushing at its face.

It growled again, but leaped out of the flour sack, shaking itself off like a dog after a bath, and sending white dust everywhere.

It started to come toward the door of the pantry, and he put his arm out over Cara, moving her to the side as the snarling beast loped out of the pantry and through the kitchen.

"And open the door," he said.

"I mean, the question is, how did it get in?"

"That's a good question, but we need to get it out first."

"He's just going to come back."

"Fine. We'll work on raccoon prevention once we've done raccoon eradication."

He went to the side door off the kitchen and propped it open with the doorstop, then took the broom and pushed it against the raccoon's rear.

It growled again, but picked up the pace, scampering out the door and disappearing into the night.

"For God's sake." He lifted up the doorstop and shut the door. "I was not expecting that."

"No. That was ridiculous."

"Really, really ridiculous," he said.

"But cute."

"It was *not* cute."

"I disagree."

"So, you might not have a ghost in the hotel, but you might have raccoons. And, we don't know how they're getting in, which is going to require some kind of a fix. This place is a death trap," he said.

"It is not a death trap. I just wish that I had evidence that it's haunted."

"You're not going to get that, because it is not haunted."

"You don't know that," she said.

"Well, the problem is, I fucking do. Because ghosts don't exist."

He was just glad to be having this argument with her, because at least he was on stable ground.

And it wasn't about… Any of the things that had happened before.

"Let's go back upstairs," he said. "We'll look for raccoon entries in the morning."

"Okay."

They had kept the movie playing, but it didn't matter, since they'd both seen it a whole bunch of times. She drank another glass of wine, and he didn't say anything, because he was actually hoping that they might just get past all that. That she might forget it had happened. And she seemed to have.

When the movie ran out, she fell asleep on the sleeping bag. And he lay back on his own. He was lying on his side, and he could see her, in the moonlight coming through the window. The gentle swells of her breasts rising and falling with each breath.

And he couldn't take his eyes off her.

She was beautiful, and he'd always known that. But...

It was like a cascade of things he had held back for any number of years were suddenly rolling through him.

He had kept any thought of her as being a woman—a woman who was available to him—entirely subdued for all these years.

And she had undone it all with that tipsy offer. Because suddenly, he couldn't stop making it real. Couldn't stop seeing it as something vivid and specific and possible. Pushing his hands up underneath her shirt and revealing her skin. Had no one ever done that? Would his hands really be the first hands to…

No. He protected her. That was what he did.

He shielded her. From hard emotions, and held her when it was all unavoidable.

And there was no way in the damned world that he could protect her if he was…

He turned over onto his side and faced away from her, desperate to do something to find a way to get his mind out of the damned gutter.

And then she made a little whimpering noise, and he sat up. He couldn't take it. He crossed the room and got up on the bed and lay down on his back. He didn't care how dusty it was.

He needed some space. He just needed some space.

Cara felt dizzy when she woke up. And she couldn't figure out why she woke up, because it was still the middle of the night.

And then suddenly, she saw what looked like a light. A floating orb in the middle of the room. It was low, at eye level with her on the ground. She sat up and looked around, and she saw that Jace wasn't on his sleeping bag. She scrambled up, her heart thundering. And then she noticed him on the bed, sleeping.

She scrambled up on the bed beside him, but he didn't move. He was snoring. "Go away," she said to the floating light. It zigzagged in the room. "Please go away. You're scaring me."

The light seemed to respond. It stopped, and then she swore she saw…that it wasn't an orb or just a light, but it was a butterfly. A bright white butterfly.

And she sat there blinking, completely uncertain of what she had seen. Maybe she just had something in front of her eyes because she was a little bit hungover or whatever from just having drunk too much wine. All she knew was that it creeped her out. She grabbed the ties on the curtains, and let them fall around the bed. She and Jace were completely boxed in there in the canopy.

She curled up in a ball and lay beside him, trying not to breathe too hard.

She just wanted to go back to sleep. And she wanted to hear nothing. So she focused on the sound of her breathing. His breathing. Tried to make it loud so that she wouldn't hear anything unnerving.

Hoped that orbs couldn't come through curtains.

She swallowed hard, trying to get a hold of herself.

And finally, she drifted off into a fitful sleep.

Six

When Cara woke up, it was dim. She squinted and realized that she was sleeping on a canopy bed. And she could see little shafts of sunlight coming through the cracks in the curtain.

Oh right. She had woken up and thought she'd seen… A ghost last night. An orb. A glowing butterfly? She had read a lot of things written by ghost hunters, and enough to know that orbs usually indicated some kind of paranormal activity. Glowing butterflies, she had no idea.

She immediately questioned that, because the fact that she knew it meant that it was something that had been suggested to her prior to being here. Which meant she could easily have dreamed it, freaked out and…

She turned to look at Jace, who was asleep in bed beside her.

And everything in her stopped. Stopped thinking about ghosts. Stopped thinking about anything.

All she could do was stare at him. He looked a lot more relaxed sleeping. Way more relaxed than he ever did in person. In person he always looked like he was ready to leap into action. At any moment. To vanquish a raccoon or...

Oh no. There was a raccoon.

Last night had gotten very strange, and it was all a little bit fuzzy, because she had been drunk. She'd had way too much wine because she was nervous. But yes, they heard a noise and it had turned out that it was a raccoon. They'd gone downstairs, Jace had vanquished the raccoon...well, he had scuttled out of the room...

But something had happened before that.

But she was stopped again by the sight of him. His profile.

By everything. Just everything.

She took a deep breath. And the scent of him was almost overwhelming. Then she suddenly felt a little bit creepy, sitting there and staring at him like that. Checking him out. She sat up, pulling her knees up to her chest, and her head gave a decisive, definitive dull thud.

Great. And she had a hangover.

If you wanted to have sex with a virgin, you could have sex with me.

She slapped her hand over her mouth.

No.

She had not said that. She really needed that to be a dream, or just something she had thought, or just…

If she could see it clearly. Play back that whole conversation. Everything that had happened right before the raccoon… The raccoon had interrupted the conversation. She had literally *propositioned* Jace and had told him that she *was a virgin.*

She squeezed her hands even more tightly over her mouth to keep from whimpering out loud.

No. And now she was up here in bed with him, and he was going to think that she was… That she had lost her mind.

I promise I'm not trying to hit on you. It's just that I saw a ghost. And I freaked out.

Yeah. That would go well. Just great.

Her heart was thundering out of control. Was he going to say something? Was he going to call her out for hitting on him? Was he going to ask about her virginity? Oh, she could think of nothing more embarrassing. It was a literal horror. The idea that he knew… No.

She couldn't bear it. She really couldn't bear it.

But maybe he wouldn't remember. He had a little bit of wine himself. And they'd made it through the night in the haunted house. Which was… Pretty haunted. Except maybe that it had been a dream. Because she'd been drunk.

She really didn't know what to think. She didn't know what to hope for.

And suddenly, he made a very masculine noise and stirred in his sleep. And then he turned over and looked at her, and she felt like the whole world lit up.

He was the most beautiful thing she'd ever seen. It hurt to look at him.

You love him.

No. She really didn't need to think that. She tried not to think it. She tried to never, ever think it. Yes, she loved him. As a friend, almost a brother, really. But the feelings…the attraction feelings… Those things she tried to keep separate and in their own box. Desire didn't have to be anything deeper.

But right now, lying next to him in bed, it was hard to keep it separate. They seemed to wrap around her completely, like invisible vines. Jace. And everything he was to her, along with how much she wanted to lean in and…

She rolled in the opposite direction. Fast. And went right off the edge of the mattress, down to the floor.

"Ow!"

She looked around the room, all lit up with daylight and felt…silly. About the whole ghost thing. About getting into bed with Jace…

"What happened?" She could hear him moving behind the curtain.

"I fell. I…"

"Were you up here?" he asked, and she was thankful he was behind the curtain and she was on the floor.

"Yeah I…something freaked me out last night." She winced. "So I got in bed and closed the curtains. Sorry."

"No need to apologize."

She heard his feet hit the floor on the other side of the bed, and she stood up quickly because she didn't need for him to see her on the floor in an undignified heap when she was sure she already sounded like an undignified heap. He didn't need visual confirmation.

She smoothed her hair and tried to lean casually against the bedpost. He came around the corner of the bed and she ignored the way her heart throbbed. "Morning," she said.

"You made it. The hotel is yours. Assuming you still want to buy it after Raccoonageddon."

"Oh, if anything I want it more."

"This is why you need a full-time babysitter, Cara."

"Don't worry. I'm bringing Grandpa's whiskey bottle over."

"Cara… That's not what I mean. Let's go out to the diner and get some breakfast."

And she was grateful for that. Because she needed

to get back somewhere more familiar with him. On regular old footing. He was acting normal. Unaffected. Standing there in the same jeans and Henley he'd been wearing yesterday, he almost looked like last night hadn't happened. And maybe… Maybe he didn't remember. It wasn't like they'd done anything. It was just that she'd… Told him one of her more embarrassing secrets, and… Really, it wasn't so much like she had propositioned him. She could play it off like it was a joke.

It was just… It had not been a joke. And it hurt her to know that at the very first moment, she had exposed herself like that. Why had she done that to herself? He didn't want her. If he did, there had been ample opportunity for him to let her know along the way. Not that she had really ever let him know. But… There also hadn't been anyone else.

She ignored the ache in her chest that was still there from moments ago. From that terrible, ridiculous thought about love.

She didn't need to go thinking things like that.

And she didn't need to go marinating in all these feelings. They were just Jace and Cara, the same as they'd always been. One weird moment wasn't going to change that.

They packed up their things and went back out to Jace's truck.

"If you want, I can drive us over to the diner, then swing us back by here."

"Sure," she said.

The diner was packed. It was Sunday morning, and a whole lot of people were there for free church bacon and eggs. And a lot of other people were there for a hangover cure. The diner was where every kind of person in Lone Rock met.

"Good morning," said Rosemary, who had been hostess at the diner ever since they had graduated from high school.

"Morning," said Cara.

"Two," said Jace.

Rosemary gave them a sidelong glance.

All right, they had shown up at the diner for breakfast together. But hey, they had spent the night together. It was just it wasn't like that.

It was frustrating. Knowing that everyone in town basically assumed that she and Jace were sleeping together, when they absolutely weren't.

She wanted the diner to be a normalizing moment, and in many ways, she supposed that it was, since these kinds of speculative looks were normal for them. It was just that… She wanted to not think about him that way. And there was a strange kind of intimacy that seemed to linger between them after last night.

They sat down at the booth, and Rosemary handed them the menus. "Coffee?"

"Yes," they both said at the same time.

"I have a bastard of a headache," said Jace.

"You weren't even that drunk," she pointed out.

"It's that sugary girlie wine," he said. "I can drink Jack Daniel's and feel nothing the next day."

"So what you're telling me, is that you're not man enough for girls' night."

"I am not," he said.

"Maybe your toxic masculinity is protecting you."

"I would maintain that," he said.

A few moments later, their coffee arrived.

"Do you need a minute?" Rosemary asked.

"No," said Jace. "Bacon and eggs. Over medium. Hash browns, sourdough toast."

"Same."

Rosemary nodded, then left, and both she and Jace lifted their coffee mugs up and took long drinks.

As soon as that first hit of caffeine touched her soul, she started to feel slightly more human.

"I want to invest in the hotel."

"What?"

"I was thinking. After we talked last night, about the trust fund, and all of that... I want to invest in the hotel."

"You want to invest in the hotel. And when you say that, you mean you actually want to do this, and this isn't you doing some kind of misguided older brother thing?"

She was trying to sort through the tangle of feelings that this offer brought up. There was a certain measure of relief, because having some extra financial support—especially considering that there was clearly a raccoon porthole somewhere—was great. And certainly offered her a little bit of reassurance. But then also, if he remembered that conversation from last night…

Of course, that conversation had only been a couple sips of wine in, and it had come before all the raccoon stuff, way before, meaning she hoped that what had come right before the raccoon stuff, had been swallowed up by both that and the wind.

"So you want to… You want to throw backing behind this?"

"Yeah," he said. "I do need something that I believe in. That I want to invest in. Why not the town?"

"I just can't escape the feeling that actually what you're doing is acting like a mother hen."

"I prefer older brother."

Oh well. He might as well have just taken the butter knife next to his right hand and stabbed her in the heart. Done a little dance around her body as she bled out for good measure.

"I don't need an older brother," she said, her tone crisp. "Thank you. A friend, who sees me as an equal, sure."

"Me feeling like an older brother doesn't preclude me seeing you as an equal."

But it definitely precluded him seeing her as a woman. Great. Maybe it was even worse than she was thinking. Maybe he did remember what she had said last night, and he was not surprised that she was a virgin, and also didn't take seriously her offer for him to relieve her of it at all, because why would he, because she would've had to be kidding, because obviously they weren't attracted to each other.

She was rescued by the arrival of her breakfast, and she tucked into her eggs fiercely, mixing the yolks up in her hash browns and dipping her toast in the rest.

"You okay?"

"Starving," she said.

"Yeah. All right. Anyway, I figure if you're going to go over to the bank today, maybe I can go with you. And we can maybe have me cosign the paperwork."

"I don't need you to cosign, Jace. And if you're thinking that's a way to help keep me safe or bail me out or whatever…"

"Hey, all right. If you don't want my name on the paperwork, that's fine. I really was just trying to be helpful. I promise that I'm not… Doubting you."

"Whatever your crisis is, it doesn't have anything to do with me."

"Not a crisis," he said. "I've basically lived my life this way on purpose. I don't have a lot of connections. Other than my family, and I love them. And I've got you. But I don't own property, I don't do a job where I am doing any one thing for any length of time. I got all this money that I earned riding bulls, and you tell me what's…meaningful about that? Now I'm going to get a whole bunch of money that I didn't even earn. I don't know. Part of me wants to live that way, but… At this point… It's also starting to seem a little bit pointless. And useless. You want things, and I admire that. You're right. I don't put a lot of stock in dreams. And I'm still not in a place where I want to put any in my own. Or even have any of my own. But I'm happy to invest in yours. Don't see it as anything other than that. Your dreams feel valuable to me. So…"

"Yeah," she said, her heart seizing up. "Okay."

Why was it like this? Why was he like this? It really… It really got her. Right square at the center of her chest. He was doing this for her. And not to be condescending or anything like that, just because he cared.

And she didn't know why in the hell that made him feel like he was sitting further away from her than he had been a moment before. Because it should feel like they were closer.

But there was just something… There was something. Something that was there for her that was missing for him.

And she would never be able to talk to him about it. She would never be able to bridge that gap, because he was all she had. She had made an idiot out of herself last night. But there were a ton of handsome men. A ton of them. She saw them every night at the bar. Little Rock was lousy with hot cowboys. If that was her thing, then there was ample opportunity for her to pursue that. The one thing she would never be able to replicate or re-create was this relationship with him. The one thing she would never be able to have again, with anyone else, was what she had with Jace. This long-standing, completely trusting friendship. Something that was kind of more like family, if she were honest.

And he was the only family she had left, really.

He was important to her. In ways that were so complicated and imperative, there was no untangling it all. "Okay," she said again. "I'll take your help. You can invest, but I'm going to sign the paperwork on my own."

"Fair enough. What I'd like to do is help finance the remodels then."

"All right," she said.

"Then you have yourself a partner."

"A haunted house partner," she said.

"It's not haunted by anything but raccoons."

"Still. That's pretty haunted."

She reached across the table and stuck her hand out. And only when his large, warm, calloused hand wrapped around hers completely, did she recognize the error of her ways. Yeah, maybe that wasn't the smartest thing to have done. But he was her friend; she wasn't going to just not touch him. To not shake his hand.

So she did, firmly. And then brought her hand back over to her side of the table and started shoveling more eggs into her mouth.

"I'm going to make my offer right after breakfast," she said, around her eggs. "Then I'll sign the paperwork, and then… We can make a meeting with the contractor."

"All right. Sounds good."

By the time he got back to the ranch, he almost wasn't thinking about that moment last night, over and over again. Almost.

He thought that he had done a pretty good job playing it cool this morning. But when he'd woken up, it hadn't been the raccoon that he thought of. It had been that moment when she looked at him, all glossy eyed, and told him that she was a virgin.

And that if he wanted to have sex with one…

Holy shit.

He had no idea what he was supposed to do with that.

Because he hadn't been able to get it out of his mind, and he was…

His body stirred.

Hell. And damn.

But he was resolved in his decisions to invest in the hotel. Even more so after last night. She needed him. If he didn't help, she was going to end up neck-deep in debt.

And maybe… Okay, maybe he needed her too.

Maybe he was ready to admit it was time to make something of his own.

But this was the thing. Whatever had happened last night, it was an anomaly. He wasn't going to let that dictate his actions, but it might also be telling him that he needed to stop and make a choice.

He was all thrown off because he was indecisive. So he was indecisive no more.

He was investing in the hotel. He was staying.

He'd realized this morning at breakfast that he couldn't afford to be wishy-washy. Not now. This was the time to make a decision.

He put his truck in Park and got out, stepping toward the barn. There had to be something to do. It was a ranch. There had to be something physical that he could pour himself into.

He was just about to go grab a rake, because God knew he could probably always muck a stall, when his brother Boone appeared from one of the stalls. "Howdy," he said. He looked him over. "You look… Not particularly well rested."

"What's your problem, Boone?"

"I don't have a problem. You seem to."

"No problem. Just thinking about some things."

"Oh yeah?" Boone crossed his arms over his chest and leaned against the stall door. "What kind of things?"

"I decided to invest in Cara's hotel thing."

"Her hotel thing?"

"Yes. You know, she's going to buy the Little Rock hotel. I thought that I would throw some money behind it. What she wants to do is pretty ambitious and... Anyway, I get the trust fund money next week."

"Wow. Well. Good for you. And here I thought you were just going to use it the way that I did."

"Hookers and blow?"

Boone laughed. "I mean, basically."

"I think we both know that isn't true," said Jace.

"Hey. You don't know."

"I think you pretend there's nothing more to you than that, but we all know there is."

"There maybe used to be," he said. "But there's not now." He got a slightly distant look to his eye.

It was impossible to know what Boone thought about anything. And yet, sometimes, Jace thought there was something in his brother that was just plain sad, and it wasn't the same kind of sad the rest of them were—they shared a common grief, so there was a bit of it that was inevitable. But there was something else to Boone, he just couldn't quite say what it was.

"Have you ever thought about investing in property?"

"Sounds dangerously like settling down," said Boone. "And that is also not in the cards for me."

"So you just going to... What? And I'm serious, because I'm trying to figure this out too. You just going to have all this money, and nothing to invest it in. Nothing to make your own."

Boone shrugged. "I have to find something that was worth making my own. Something that didn't belong to someone else, that is."

"Do you want something that does belong to someone else?"

"Story time's over," said Boone. And he knew that he'd hit a nerve.

"What's going on?"

"Nothing. And anyway, none of your business. But there's nothing wrong with just living life. Nothing wrong with… Hell, I mean, we've all accomplished things in the rodeo."

"Yeah. We got a bunch of belt buckles. And a bunch of money. It's just… Sometimes I ask what it's all for."

"What do you mean? It's our family legacy?"

"It's Dad's legacy," Jace said. "It's not mine. I never sat down and decided that it was something I wanted to do. I just did it. And now I guess sometimes I want something that's a little bit more… Mine."

"So that's where this hotel thing comes in?"

"I guess so."

"Well good luck to you. It still sounds an awful lot like an entanglement to me. And honestly, another thing that makes you and Cara basically married. Now you're business partners too? I don't know about that."

"Good thing is I didn't ask you," he said. "Didn't even start to. You're the one who asked. I'm just letting you know."

"Right. Well. I wish you the best of luck with that endeavor. And hopefully whatever else has you tensed up. Because something tells me it's not just that."

And then his brother left, but Jace still felt irritated. Because damn him, he was right. He was right about the fact that there was something else bothering him.

It was the fact that his body seemed to have developed an irrepressible interest in Cara.

He couldn't claim that it was sudden. It felt sudden. But it was just… He knew that she was beautiful. It was just that he had never let that matter. Because what did beauty matter? There were a lot of beautiful women. But there were very few people in his life that he cared for like he cared for her. And there was no one exactly like her. So he let all that fade to the background, and he never let it become attraction.

But there it was. Just suddenly. He was… He couldn't stop thinking about the way that she'd said that, and the inevitable thoughts that had followed.

How much he wanted…

Hell.

He wanted her.

No. He didn't have to let it go that far. He had a little bit of an interest there, but that was it. That didn't mean that he wanted her. And it didn't have to be anything too deep.

He wouldn't let it be.

In fact, tonight he would go to the bar, meet with her and talk her plans over with her. He wasn't going to let it be weird. He was just going to keep it the same. It was entirely possible Cara didn't even remember saying that to him. She hadn't acknowledged it all day. Not at all. Maybe she had even been kidding. Because he just couldn't imagine…

Except what was becoming easier and easier to imagine was his own hands skimming over her curves.

He could remember when he had pulled her down on top of them last night. How soft she'd been.

It had been a juvenile thing to do, but the feelings that had resulted had been anything but.

And then after that…

You've been tempting it. Teasing it.

He would've said no. That he'd never done that. Not with her. But the way that he had teased her last night, even before she'd said that to him about her virginity… It made him wonder. It made him wonder what he was actually thinking.

He needed to get back on the road, maybe. Maybe that was the issue. He'd been home a long time. And after school, for most of their friendship, they had gotten some decent-sized breaks from one another while he went out on the rodeo. And he usually hooked up when he went out on the rodeo. Quite a bit.

He didn't like the way that thought made him feel. Like it was only having sex with other women that kept him from being attracted to her.

That it was only some weird dry spell now that made him feel different.

He felt like it cheapened what they had between them, and like it cheapened her a bit, and nothing about Cara was cheap. He gritted his teeth and tried to get a grip.

Yeah. Tonight he would make sure that things got back to normal. And pretty soon that little snippet of conversation would fade into the background. It would just become one of the many conversations they'd had, and it wouldn't stand out as being anything more than what had gone on before it.

Just a snippet of things they'd said to each other.

It didn't have to echo in his mind. It didn't have to echo in his body. It really didn't.

So he took one more shovelful of manure and relished the ache in his arms.

He was going to work until he was busted. Then he was going to go have a drink with his best friend. And make some plans for the new business venture.

It wasn't like being married. Because being married wasn't in the cards for him. Not ever.

But this? This felt better. This felt right. This felt

like he was getting close to doing the thing that he needed to do. Because something had to change. He wasn't going to turn thirty and just stay the same old way. Boone might be comfortable with that, but Jace wasn't.

And this was the right step forward. He knew it.

So he banished anything that felt wrong and kept on shoveling.

Seven

By the time Jace stumbled into The Thirsty Mule with two of his brothers, he was pretty damned tired. Which was exactly what he wanted. He wanted to be bone-tired by the time he hit his bed tonight. And he definitely didn't want to think. He saw Cara standing behind the bar, glowing. She was lit up like a firecracker. Laughing and talking to two men sitting in front of her who were… Looking down her top.

And suddenly, Jace couldn't look away. Not from down her top, though his eyes definitely drifted there. But just from her. Altogether.

Her blond hair was lit up like a halo, and she looked so damned happy. She had on makeup tonight. Dark mascara and glossy pink lipstick. There was a glow about her cheeks, and he had a feeling she dusted some kind of sparkling powder on there.

And yeah… If he wasn't mistaken, she had put a bit of it on her breasts…

"Damn. She is pretty."

That came from Flint.

Jace scowled. "Shut the fuck up."

"Down boy," said Boone.

"Well. If you guys could stop being perverts about my best friend for five minutes, that would really help. You treat her like an object, and I'm sick of it."

"To be clear, when we tease you about her," said Boone, "it has nothing to do with her, and everything to do with you. Right now has a bit to do with her. Because damn."

The problem was, he couldn't even disagree. But it didn't feel like objectifying her. Not really. It felt like something else. Something different. It felt like something singular, like something had reached up and grabbed him by the throat and shaken him hard. And he didn't like it. No, he really didn't. Worst of all, his brothers were there. Worst of all, there was a bar full of people. If there wasn't…

He could see it clearly. Going over to the bar and leaning over, hooking his arm around her waist and…

No. What the hell? She was supposed to be like a sister to him. She was…

There was something unraveling here, and he couldn't quite put a finger on it. And maybe it had to do with all this need to reframe his life. With all these thoughts he had about what he wanted to do with his life and himself. Maybe he was looking for something to hold on to, and there she was.

Hell. She'd always been the thing he'd held on to.

Maybe that was what he was doing now. Just so desperate to find something that he…

He gritted his teeth and went to the empty barstool and sat down. Boone and Flint sat on either side of him.

Cara whipped her head to the side, and the moment that she saw him… There was something on her face, and he couldn't quite read it. But it reminded him of the sun coming up from behind the mountains. It reminded him of some kind of beauty he never considered before. Something that had never been spoken about or written about or even sung about. And he was not a poet by nature. But there was something that stirred inside of his soul that defied words and poetry. Something that made him feel unworthy. Of standing there. Of looking at her.

Of being in this spot.

He looked up behind her, at the Jack Daniel's bottle there that contained Mitch.

And he didn't believe in that sort of thing, but he had to wonder if the old man knew somehow. Maybe he'd just put a hex on him. Left a spell behind here in the bar that would affect any man that ever looked at Cara.

Why was that less insane than thinking he might be here now? He couldn't say.

Except he'd always been pretty clear within himself that… That the end was the end.

But hoping for anything else was just trying to put a Band-Aid on the pain that life brought.

He was resistant to Band-Aids. He preferred to rub a little dirt in it and get on with things.

Yeah. You get on with things so well. You're thirty years old and have no idea what you want.

"Can we get a drink?"

His voice came out harsh, and he felt bad, because he sure as hell didn't need to talk to her that way. Especially not when she just looked at him like that. Her expression fell, and he felt like a dick.

"Yeah." She had recovered quickly, grinning like he was just another bar patron. She often did that. It was part of the show, after all. She didn't break character when she was behind the bar.

She moved over and put her hand on her hip. "Boone? Flint? What can I get for you?"

"Something strong," said Flint.

"I drew the short straw," said Boone. "I'm driving. So I'll just have a beer."

"I know what you like," she said to Jace.

And the words felt like a swipe of her tongue, straight down the center of his chest.

And that was a weird and graphic metaphor that he'd certainly never thought before. Not about her.

"She knows what you like," said Boone.

"I could know what you like too, Boone. If you'd let me."

"Shit," Jace said. "It's bad enough that they pull this kind of stuff to make me mad. Now you're in on it?" he asked.

Cara looked at him blandly, then shrugged. "What's the harm in it?"

"God Almighty," said Jace. "You're all going to be the death of me."

She winked at Boone. *Winked* at him.

"Well," said Boone. "Never mind. I take back everything I said about you practically being married to her. She's obviously single."

"Really, are you just trying to make me mad?"

"Why are you so mad?" Flint asked.

And the problem was, he didn't have an answer. Not a good one. Not a good one at all.

"I want a burger," he said. "If you're done flirting with my brother."

"Yeah, I'm done," Cara said. "For now."

She walked back down the bar, and he couldn't help but watch the wiggle of her hips, the way her ass looked in those jeans.

It was like the floodgates had opened, and now that he had noticed, he couldn't stop.

If you want to have sex with a virgin...

She couldn't be a virgin. She just couldn't be. And it wasn't because he didn't believe she was capable of making that choice, he just didn't... She exuded sex appeal. She was so comfortable with herself. With her body. The way that she handled the men in the room was… She had them all eating out of the palm of her hand. She just seemed like a woman who was *experienced*. He had accepted that. He didn't really ever think about it. They didn't talk about that sort of thing. That was fine. It wasn't part of their friendship. They were sort of open…

And now that he thought about it, he couldn't remember her ever dating anybody, but the thing was, he was gone sometimes. And anyway, he figured that she probably had her share of hookups working at the bar and…

He looked at all the men sitting around the bar. The thought of any of them putting their hands on her made him so angry he couldn't even see straight.

She leaned forward and started talking to two men down at the other end. They were getting an eyeful down her tank top, and the thing was, he knew that she knew it. And that if she didn't want them to, she wouldn't hold herself in that position. She was a woman in total control of herself. She knew exactly the effect that she had on men, and she was happy to have it.

He just couldn't see…

But maybe that was his own wrongheaded thinking.

Maybe it showed what he knew about anything.

It was almost funny. That there was something he

didn't know about Cara Summers. That there was maybe something he didn't understand about women.

And hell, sitting there looking at her like he was, he wondered if there were some things he maybe didn't understand about himself. And that was a whole other Pandora's box of freaky-ass shit he didn't want to open.

His brothers and his burgers arrived a few moments later, along with their drinks, and he did his best to listen to Boone talk about his plans for the next rodeo season.

His plans to get on the road.

Flint had similar plans. And he realized just none of it… Resonated in him. Not anymore.

He shoved down his french fries.

"I think I'm going to stay here," he said.

"Really?" Boone asked. "You're not going back out there?"

"I want everything. I've made tons of money. It's time for me to figure out the next thing. I need something that's… I need something that's mine."

Right when he said that, he looked back behind the bar, and his eyes connected with Cara's and, on God, he had not meant for that to happen. But it had, and it resonated down deep inside of him. Made him feel something he really wished he hadn't.

"I mean, more power to you," said Boone. "But I'm not done with the glory."

"I mean, I could do with a little bit less infamy," Flint mused.

Boone snorted. "It'll pass," he said. "Nobody's going to remember that Tansey Martin wrote a song for you in another year."

"It's not about me," said Flint, practically growling.

"It's not? Because I seem to recall…"

"She didn't love me," said Flint. "If she had, I would've known."

"You think so?" Boone asked.

"Yeah," said Flint. "I think so. It was nothing."

And Jace didn't quite believe that. And maybe it was asinine of him, but he kind of liked the fact that his brother wasn't really as certain about things as he tended to pretend.

Boone and Flint were not as gloriously unattached as they pretended. Commentary from the last couple of days had shown him that.

Of course, that didn't really help much. It only made him wonder if he'd ever been as detached as he pretended. If he'd been lying to himself as well as he ever had to anyone else.

They finished their burgers, and Boone downed another shot, simply because he could.

"Let's go," Flint said. "I'm bored of sitting here sober."

"See you later," said Jace. "I'm going to hang out for a bit."

It was getting crowded in the bar, and he didn't like the idea of leaving. Not with Cara looking like that. Not with all these men here staring at her.

You just want to keep staring at her.

She was his friend. It was more than that. It would always be more than that.

His brothers left, and he kept his position at the bar. Kept it until things started to fade out. Until Cara rang the bell for last call.

Until the very last patron exited the bar, and they were the only two people left inside.

"I'm going to need a ride home," he said.

He wasn't drunk. All the whiskey had left his system a couple hours earlier. He wished he were a little drunk.

"Weird," she said. "I don't seem to recall agreeing to that."

"I figured you probably wouldn't leave me here."

"Well, that's where maybe you don't know everything about me."

It was on the tip of his tongue to say that he knew more about her than he had a week ago. That he knew more about her than he wished he did.

But he was trying to get them back on equal footing.

It was tough. It was damn tough when she was standing there looking like she did. When she was looking like the embodiment of…

He cut that thought off.

He was about to think that his best friend looked like the embodiment of sex.

And that was not what he wanted to be thinking. Not now. Not ever.

"I figured we would talk a little more. About the hotel."

"Oh great," she said, leaning back against the bar. She arched her back slightly, and he couldn't help but notice the way that her breasts thrust upward.

He looked away.

"What are your plans."

"Well. That kind of all depends. On how deep of an investment you're talking about here."

He looked back at her, because even though he was feeling off-kilter at the moment, he would damn sure make eye contact with Cara when he was talking about business. When he was talking about things that mattered. "The thing is, I have more than enough. I've never been one to sit around and be idle. The rodeo might not have been my dream, but if I was going to do something, that I was going to be the best at it."

He cleared his throat. "When you have brothers who are determined to be the best at all the same things… Well, it gets a little bit competitive. And on the youngest. So I came after them. And everything they did, I wanted to have done, done better. Every record they had broken, I wanted to come up behind them and break it too. As you pointed out, I'm not a big visualizer. I'm not a dreamer."

He looked down at his hands. It was high time he did something with those hands. Built something. Made something. And doing it for Cara...that just made sense. "I just put one foot in front of the other. I live in the moment. Because of that... I went. There's no room for nerves to creep in. No room for anxiety. No room for what-ifs. And the point of all that is, I made a lot of money doing that. I'm proud of that money. Because it's mine. The money that I'm getting from the trust fund? It isn't. It's not mine. That comes from my dad. It comes from everything that he built. And the more I think about it, the more I want to invest in something permanent with it. Because I have it, whether I feel like I have a right to it or not. So. The budget's big. Did you want an in-ground pool?"

She laughed. "No. I don't think I need a pool. But... I don't really know what to do with this offer. I don't... We're friends, and I know that you care about me. You always have. But this..."

"It's a business decision. I mean, I expect a cut of it. But at least then I'm working for it. No?"

"For a man who claims he doesn't think ahead... You sure have a plan."

"Look. I just don't..." He looked at her, at the hopeful expression on her face. The glitter in her eyes. "Forget about it," he said.

"Forget about what?"

"Forget I was gonna say anything. It's not anything that we need to talk about."

"I want to talk about it. Tell me. Tell me what's going on."

"All right. You know, when somebody that you love is dying, thinking ahead just means thinking to a future without them. And I never could muster up a belief in miracles. So I just knew that if I imagined what I wanted to be when I grew up… I would be imagining a world without Sophia in it. It's a habit. All right. It's a habit that I never got around to breaking."

It was one reason he was all or nothing. In the moment and never in the future. Black-and-white was easy, and he'd lived a black-and-white life. He'd known there would be a before and an after. Sophia here. Sophia gone. There were no shades of gray in loss.

He found there weren't really any shades of gray in life.

Those glittering eyes went liquid.

"Jace…"

"It's been a long time. I don't live in the past. That's the other thing. You learn to live in the present, and she can't… You can't go back there either."

"Well that's pretty sad. Because even though she's gone, she is your sister. And maybe it would be nice if you could revisit her."

"She's gone."

"I don't believe that the people we love are ever really gone, Jace," she said. She looked back at the bar, up at the bottle that held her grandfather's ashes. "You know I talked to Grandpa every day. He's with me. I believe that."

"Well. Sophia's not with me. She's gone. One day, she just died. And she was never with me again. That's all I know."

And he didn't know why he had always felt so hard-line about that. So rigid. Maybe because if there were miracles to be had in the world, if divine power existed at all, and it had not extended its hand to keep Sophia with him, physically with him, then he didn't see the point of it anyway. And frankly it was a bigger comfort to believe there was just nothing there. That was all.

Maybe some people preferred the comfort of faith. He didn't find it comforting. He didn't find it comforting to think that there was someone who could've lifted a finger to save her, and hadn't.

He didn't find it comforting to think that somebody might be there in spirit when he couldn't actually talk to them.

And he didn't like to think about any of this. Because there was no damned point to it. None whatsoever. It didn't accomplish anything. Didn't fix anything.

He didn't know why she was pushing.

"I'm sorry that I never met her," she said.

He thought back to the boy he'd been when he had met Cara. "Well, you and I never would've met when she was alive. Because we had to live in Portland as long as she was sick. Make sure she was near the hospital."

"I know. I'm just talking about what-ifs."

"I don't get the point of those."

"Not even a little? Like you never ask yourself... What might happen if you set your foot on a different path? This one or that one?" She looked up at him, and her blush pink lips parted. She drew in a breath, and her breasts lifted.

Fuck. Right then, he wanted to ask what if. Wanted to ask what would happen if he stepped on a different path. But to what end?

Since when do you care about the end?

One foot in front of the other. Just as far as the eye could see. And no farther.

If a man was meant to see beyond the horizon, there wouldn't be a line.

But there was. Firmly drawn. You weren't meant to look ahead too far.

And right now, it was easy to believe that there was nothing outside of this bar. The thing outside of this moment. It was how he felt when he got on the back of a bull.

There was nothing but that. But his thighs pressed against the bull's flanks. The breathing of the animal as he prepared for the chute to open. For the fight to begin. The rush of adrenaline in his own body as he prepared for the fight of his life.

Those were the moments in life he loved, because they narrowed down to fractions of a second. To a single moment.

To everything.

Everything being within reach. Everything being within sight.

There was simply his hand wrapped around the leather strap, the sensation of that pressure pushing the glove more deeply into his palm. The smell of the dust and the animal. The sound of Garth Brooks and the crowd.

This moment was like that. Suddenly, there was nothing. Nothing but her. Nothing but him. Even the edges of the room had gone dark and fuzzy.

The jukebox was playing Luke Bryan. The room smelled like alcohol, fry oil and tobacco. And she looked like heaven. Something bright and glowing against the darkened backdrop.

And there was no moment beyond this one. Nothing beyond the next breath.

And nothing, nothing beyond the last breath.

And so it seemed the easiest thing in the world to take a step toward her. And then another. The easiest thing in the world to square his body right in front of hers, and watch as she pressed herself just slightly against the bar. Away from him, but her eyes told him that she didn't actually want to move farther away.

And then her eyes dropped to his mouth, back up to his eyes. And if he were to ask what they were doing, he wouldn't have an answer. If he were to ask himself why the hell he was about to do this, he wouldn't have an answer.

But he just didn't need an answer. He didn't need a fucking answer. Because that meant that there was something beyond this. And right now he wasn't acknowledging that. Not even a little bit.

It was only this. Only this.

And that was when he planted his hands on the edge of the bar, on either side of her body, and looked at her like he might be able to find some answers at the very bottom of that green gaze.

She lifted one hand and placed it on his chest. Warm fingertips flexing there, shifting the fabric of his shirt over his skin. His heart rate kicked up, like he was about to ride, and the world narrowed even further. Pink cheeks, pink lips, green eyes.

She looked up at him from beneath her lashes and leaned in. He felt her breath against his skin. Then she moved her hand to the back of his neck. Her fingertips were so soft. Impossibly.

Cara shifted, leaned in, stretched up on her toes.

And she kissed him.

Eight

Oh, she was doing it. She was kissing him. Her mouth brushed his, and a streak of heat went through her that she couldn't deny. She pulled away, almost the instant their mouths touched. "I'm sorry," she said. She turned away. "Shit. I'm sorry," she said again.

He grabbed her arm and turned her to face him, his hands curved around her forearms, and gripping the edge of the bar, pinning her there. "You just kissed me."

"I did," she said.

And suddenly, she found herself being hauled toward him, and he wrapped his arm around her waist, pushing her body against his, and when he kissed her, he did not move away.

No. His kiss was deep, hard. Hot.

And it was Jace.

She wanted to pull away and scream with the hysteria of it.

Jace.

It was Jace.

And he was kissing her. His lips were firm and expert, and then he angled his head, and she opened her mouth to him. And his tongue slid against hers. Jace's tongue.

And she was trembling. Immediately wet between her legs. Because her fantasies had primed her for this moment over the course of years, and yet it was so much better than she had ever imagined that it could be.

This kiss was beyond anything that she had ever fathomed a kiss might be. He was everything. And too much all at once. So tall and strong and hot. All-knowing. Like he was demanding a response from her. Like he was willing it from the depths of her soul.

And she couldn't doubt. Because how could she, when she was being kissed by a man who so clearly knew exactly what he was doing. A man who didn't seem to have doubt anywhere in his body, anywhere at all. And she would know, since she was currently plastered against his body.

He pulled her away from him, and looked down at her. "Are you really a virgin?"

"Well. I thought we weren't talking about that."

"You *kissed* me, Cara."

"You also kissed me. So I think we're even."

"Not even a little bit. Were you serious?"

"Was I serious?" She squinted, and tried to look confused.

"You are not fucking confused. You know exactly what I mean. Were you serious?"

"Yeah," she said, realizing that it was all futile now. And if she got weird about it, it was only going to be weirder. If she pretended, after kissing him like that and then returning his kiss like he was oxygen and she was suffocating to death, it was only going to look more extreme. More ridiculous.

So there was just a point where she was going to have to exhibit some honesty. "I was serious. Yes. I haven't ever been with anyone. And you know, it's one of those things… That at this point it's kind of weird and left undone, and if you would like to be the one to help me out with it, then I am okay with it. It just has to be the one…the once. I appreciate the fact that you're already helping me with my hotel. And it might be a little bit much to ask you to pay for renovation and also have sex with me."

Well. She wanted to crawl under the bar. She had just said all those words to Jace, and she wasn't even drunk. She couldn't blame them on anything like that. Couldn't take refuge in the fact that she was maybe being an idiot.

"You're a virgin?"

"Yes."

"And you would like to not be." He said it not so much as a question, but as a clarifying statement.

Though in general, that wasn't true. If she had actually wanted to lose her virginity, if it were even a thing to her, then she would've done it. It was just that she… She was stuck in some kind of weird limbo with Jace.

Weird limbo. Weird way to say: you're in love with him.

Hell. She didn't want to think about being in love with Jace. The very thought made her want to cry. She didn't want to be in love with Jace. It was fucking stupid. She did not want to be in love with Jace.

But as she stood there, looking at him, at that precious, dear, familiar, wonderful face, she knew it was true. And it was why she had never been with anyone else. Because there was just nobody that made her feel even a fraction of what he did. Because being with somebody else would be a mockery of what they had. Because it wouldn't come close to what she actually wanted it to.

"I want you," she whispered.

She wished her voice was stronger. She wished it wasn't so small.

And it was so far from the whole truth that it made her want to laugh. And it was so desperately inadequate that it made her want to cry. And so exposing that she wanted to cover herself. But looking at him, she could see the promise of something. Like the sun rising, flooding the moment with hope. With light.

And what if… What if she could have everything with him?

It was a bright, brilliant moment, but she let herself have it. Even though she didn't think it was realistic. Even though she didn't think it would ever… Ever amount to anything… She let herself dream. If only for a second. She let herself dream, because it felt right. She let herself dream, because sometimes dreams were all you had. And they were beautiful, and magical, and you should hang on to them when you could.

And who knew if she could actually have everything with Jace. She'd never been all that special.

Except to him.

But then, she also knew that he was a difficult bastard. Who didn't have a romantic bone in his body.

He didn't do long term, or even an exclusive kind of short term. Yeah, she also knew that.

"You want me?" His voice was rough and she felt it between her legs.

What was she doing? What was happening right now? He was her friend. Her best friend. Hers. And she was just telling him, and he was looking at her like he might want her too, and she wanted to run. From him and to him.

She cleared her throat. "Is that not apparent?"

He cut her off by pressing his mouth to hers, and

a rush of warmth overtook her. He wrapped his arm around her waist and brought her close. And when he kissed her… It was deep. It was real, and it was the most full-on, intense moment of its kind that she imagined anyone had ever experienced. She didn't want to talk. She didn't want to think. She didn't want to do anything but feel. She just wanted to feel. Feel this. Feel him.

She wanted it more than anything.

And she had to laugh, because she sort of wondered if they were being utterly themselves in this moment. If she was trying to manifest forever while he deeply denied any sort of future.

But maybe it didn't matter, because their truth and their beliefs were coming together right in this moment, and it was resulting in a kiss, so… She supposed that was all perfect.

And maybe she would take a page out of his book. Just this once. Because the scrape of his stubble against her cheek was magic, and the slick friction of his tongue against hers was doing wild and reckless things to her insides. Because the feel of his big hands, gripping her waist, smoothing down her hip. Oh, it was her fantasy. Her moment. It was the thing… It was everything.

She started to shake.

And he was Jace, so he noticed.

"You okay?" he asked, brushing his hand over her cheek.

"I'm okay," she said. "I just… I watched you once. Pick up a woman in the bar. The way that you put your hand on her body… I went home and I fantasized about it."

"Fuck," he said. "Don't tell me things like that."

"Why? We're already here."

He huffed a laugh, soft and sexy, and then he smiled. Just a little. "Well. Damned if that isn't true."

And then he kissed her again, and she was drowning.

She pushed her hands up underneath his T-shirt and groaned when she made contact with his hot skin. With his hard-packed muscle.

She started to pull off his shirt.

"Look, as much as I think it would be fun to do this on the bar, I think that we need to bed."

"What?"

"Seriously. You've really never been with anybody?"

"Yes." She moved her hands over his chest. "I've never been with anybody, and I want to be with you, and I'm feeling a little bit desperate."

"And there will be time for hard and fast, I can assure you. I'm all for it. But, we need to do slow and thorough first. Because I take care of you. Bottom line. You're mine, Cara. Mine to protect. And I'm gonna make this good for you. And that means we need to bed. And we need time."

"I'm a virgin," she said. "But I am not an *untouched* virgin. I have a vibrator."

"Praise the Lord, and hallelujah. But, I still want to take my time."

"I just mean… I actually know when I'm about to come. And believe me when I tell you…"

"Save the dirty talk," he said, pressing his thumb against her lips. "We're gonna have me coming a whole lot earlier than either of us want."

It was the fact that he made eye contact with her when he said that that nearly sent her over the edge. The fact that it was Jace.

Her Jace.

The fact that she had looked up and seen him down by the riverbed when she'd been crying when she was just in middle school, and he looked at her with those same eyes. And now he was looking at her like this, talking to her like that.

It was enough to send her straight over the edge.

Jace. This was *Jace*. And she didn't even have to tell herself that to cement it in her mind, because it could only ever be him.

She had been waiting for this. All this time.

"Well. We can go back to… To the house."

The house that she had inherited from her grandfather wasn't that far out of town.

"Yeah we can."

"It's convenient, since you don't even have your truck here."

"Yeah," he said, his voice ragged. "If I were a different man, I'd be tempted to say that I planned it this way. But you're you, so I definitely shouldn't of done that. And I'm me, so I'm not supposed to… Plan."

"Did you?"

"I'm not going to lie to you. What you said about that got to me. I try to not think of you that way. And when I say try, I mean I decided not to, so I didn't. You must know that you're beautiful."

"I know that men respond to me a certain way. I don't know that I think that is beautiful."

"Well you are. You're basically a damn sunrise. All right? I'm not good at that."

"That's a lie. You pick up women all the time. You must be very good at flattering them."

"I'm good at empty flattery. I'm good at letting those words roll off my lips without even thinking about what they mean. Hey gorgeous. Hey baby. You look beautiful. Like a dress. But it would look better on my bedroom floor."

She blanched. "Please tell me you've never said that."

"I probably have. I probably didn't even pay attention to what it really sounded like. But I guarantee you that neither did she. Because we were both there for one reason, and it didn't matter if we liked each other. It didn't matter. It's the perfect kind of hookup for a man like me. Who doesn't think about tomorrow." His voice pitched lower, and she shivered. "And you know, even though I don't think about my tomorrows, Cara, I know one thing about them. You'll be there. And that matters to me. It matters a hell of a lot."

Her throat went so tight she could hardly speak. "It matters to me too."

"So what I say to you matters. I'm not to give you empty compliments. And maybe that wasn't a great one, but I meant it. I meant it all away from my soul. I promise you that. You're beautiful, and I had to put blinders on to not notice. I did a pretty bad job of it when you first... Filled out."

She laughed, which felt good. "Diplomatic," she said.

"Tonight, I was watching those men look at you... And seeing you the way that they did... Well, it made me want to strangle them, but it also made it impossible to look away from you. But I want to make it very clear it's not like I didn't notice. You don't have the kind of beauty a man doesn't notice."

"Thank you," she said. "But we don't need to talk."

Because it they kept talking, then maybe she would have to share more about what she felt. Maybe she would have to share more about the way that she felt about him. The way that she had always felt about him.

"Take me home and make me feel good." And it wasn't the smoothest thing, but it was real. It was raw and it was honest. And he seemed to find it undeniable. Because that was when he grabbed her arm and led her out the back door of the bar.

And it was her truck that they needed to take, but she fumbled around looking for the keys, and finally he took pity on her and fished them out of her purse for her and got into the driver's seat.

Her house was a modest one, on one of the streets just a couple of blocks from the bar. All the houses on the street had been built in 1974. All of them the same sort of small and nondescript, or at least they had been originally. Some had been added onto over the years. Made a little bit more fancy a little bit more spacious. But not hers.

It was still the same as when she had lived here with her grandpa. The same green shag carpet. The same daisy pattern countertop in the bathroom.

She loved it because it reminded her of him. Because it reminded her of home.

Jace was a lot like home too, and somehow, right now the combination of the two didn't feel comforting. It simply felt dangerous.

They had spent the night together, shared a bed back at the motel, but this was different. It was different, and so were they.

And she fought against the thought that argued with that. That told her they were just the same. And doing this was risky. As risky as it ever had been. And she needed to be careful. So goddamned careful. And she was taking a risk because she wanted to touch him so badly.

But the fact of the matter was, the horse had bolted. They could turn back now, and things would still be different forever.

Because the acknowledgment of the feelings was the horse in the room. And the sex didn't have to actually happen for it to have been spoken of. And they'd already kissed. So there was no point turning back. Because if it was going to break something, then they'd broken it back at the bar. Maybe they'd broken it back at the hotel.

Maybe they'd broken it at some other point along the path that she couldn't even identify.

Maybe it had shattered for her the moment she had seen him put his hand on that woman's hip and envied her. Maybe that was the point from which she had been too far gone to go back.

And so she really had to be like Jace this moment. And just go forward.

But not look too far ahead.

He got out of the truck and took her keys and unlocked the front door.

She walked in first, and the very familiar room suddenly didn't look so familiar. It looked foreign and a little bit frightening, or maybe that was just her own body right now.

Foreign and a little bit frightening. Not at all what she was used to. Not at all what she expected.

And then he closed the door behind them and locked it, and suddenly it all felt so real.

She was hyperaware of everything. The sound of her breathing. The sound of the forced air coming through the vents as the heater came on. The sound of his footsteps as he walked toward her.

"Jace," she whispered.

"Cara."

It was in affirmation. That he was well aware of who she was. That he saw her. That he wanted her too.

And that was what she really needed to know. More than anything.

"This isn't just the virginity thing, is it? It's not just a novelty for you?"

"I've never found anything about virginity novel. I don't care about it. But I do care about you. I care about what you want. And you waited a long time to do this and… I want it to be good for you. So no. I don't care about that. What I care about is you. That's it. Beginning and end of story. It's you, Cara. You're what matters."

She felt like her heart was being peeled, layer by layer, like all the resistance that she had left was being stripped away. And she really didn't have much. And yet it was brutal. Utterly brutal. She hadn't expected this. That a moment so deeply desired. So anticipated, could be quite so uncomfortable.

But it was like he knew. Right then. Like he knew

just what to do. He leaned in and kissed her. And he made it impossible for her to think. And that was just exactly what she needed. A reprieve. And that was what he excelled at. She could see the appeal. Why he lived the way that he did. She could see why it felt great to block out everything but the moment. Absolutely everything.

And so she let his kiss carry her away. Or maybe keep her grounded. To the spot instead of the moments that would follow. The moments where he would see her. Touch her. Tease her in a way that no other man ever had.

Yes. She kept herself in this moment, so she wasn't quite up ahead to those.

His hands were strong and certain as he gripped her waist, rooted her to the spot, to the moment.

Her heart began to throb, her body aching with need.

It was just so good. And it surpassed everything. Every single one of her fantasies. Every single one of those illicit evenings she'd spent thinking about his hands on her body. The reality was so much sweeter. So much better.

And then suddenly, she wanted to see him. Because after all, it was her fantasy. Because after all, she was the virgin.

She pushed her hands up beneath his shirt, and he took the hint, reaching behind his head and gripping the back of his T-shirt, pulling it up over his head in a way that left her mouth ajar.

"How do men do that?"

"What?"

"I dunno. It was just the sexiest thing I've ever seen." At least, it was. It was the sexiest thing she had ever seen until she saw his body. His broad shoulders, his pectoral muscles, with just the right amount of hair sprinkled over them, his lean waist, his corrugated abs.

She licked her lips. She had seen him shirtless any number of times, but this was the first time that it had been okay for her to touch. She could touch him now.

It wasn't inappropriate for her to do that. Because he wanted this. He wanted her.

She reached out and pressed her hand against his chest. It was so hot, and she could feel his heartbeat raging there.

She was actually touching him. His skin. His body.

She hadn't done that, because they were friends. And you didn't do that to your friend. Except she was. And he was still her friend. Every bit as much as he had been before. Before she had touched him. Before everything.

He was still her friend.

She looked at him, searching his face, and suddenly, she couldn't find that assurance there. Because he looked like a stranger just then. There was something about the tension in his expression, the sharpness in his eyes. She had never seen that look on his face before. She wondered how many other women had.

But you have this other part of him. And no one else has that.

It was true. And she knew it. They had a connection, and it was bigger than this. Right then, she needed to expand the moment. To include their past.

It made her heartbeat settle just a little bit.

She continued to move her hands over his muscles, slowly, between his pecs, down to his abs, where she let her fingers drift over the ridges there. She swallowed hard. And she looked back up at him.

"What should I do?"

"Whatever you want."

"Well… I don't know what I want. Could you… Can you take control, please?"

And it was like a blue spark flashed in his eyes. It was like everything shot off like a rocket. An explosion between them.

She had felt safe with Jace, all this time, for all these years, and just now, it was like she was poised on the knife's edge of danger. Like she could see there were vast dimensions to this man that she didn't know, had never known. It was more than just tension in his face. She had opened the door and discovered vast rooms of Jace that she had never realized were there.

And he was the key to her opening the door to those rooms inside of herself too.

She just knew.

But it wasn't only that she was discovering all this about him, she was about to learn a whole lot about herself.

This was terrifying. It really was.

And wonderful too. Amazing. Something more than she had ever imagined possible. Something different.

And her fantasies about Jace hadn't prepared her. Because those were her fantasies. It was her hand on her body. Directing the tempo, directing the speed. Deciding exactly what happened when.

She had just turned the control over to him, and that meant to surrender.

On a level she had never quite dreamed.

"Are you sure?" he asked, his voice rough.

"Yes."

"If there's something I do, and you don't like it, you need to tell me to stop."

"I will." But she couldn't imagine him doing anything she didn't like. That was actually what scared her. That she wasn't sure there were going to be easy limits to this. Because discovering that he wanted her, and further, discovering that she wanted badly to surrender to whatever that meant...

It was like being tossed into the deep endlessness of the sea.

She wasn't sure it had an end.

"I want this," she said. "I want… I want you."

He growled, closed the distance between them and gripped her hands in one of his, effortlessly pinning her wrists behind her back, low, pressed against the dip in her spine right above her rear.

"Good."

The word was hard.

Final. Firm.

She loved it.

And what she loved even more was that taking care of her didn't look like being easy on her.

She didn't want easy. Because nothing had been easy to get to this point. So why should it be easy now? She just wanted to revel in this. In him.

Jace.

Her best friend with the stranger's eyes.

He kissed her, deep and fierce and hard. And then he trailed the line of kisses down her neck, to her collarbone, on down farther.

Her tank top was low, and when his lips made contact with the plump skin of her breast, she froze. It felt so good. So good. His mouth was hot, and everything in her was blooming with desire.

She had been ready to come from his kiss back at the bar, and this was… This was more extreme. More intense.

He reached down and grabbed the hem of her tank

top, pulled it up over her head, leaving her standing there in her black lacy push-up bra.

"Holy hell, Cara. You are really something else."

His eyes were appreciative, hungry, and there was no amount of male appreciation, or compliments, that would ever equal this moment. This moment when Jace Carson looked at her with lust in his eyes.

She had the sudden, ridiculous thought, that this was the highest purpose her breasts had ever had.

And it made her eager for what came next. Not nervous. But before she could unhook her bra, he reached behind her and did it, releasing it and casting it onto the ground. Her nipples went tight underneath his intense scrutiny.

She shivered.

"You are so fucking beautiful," he said, pressing a kiss to her collarbone, down farther, capturing one nipple between his teeth and tugging hard.

"Jace," she said, pushing her fingers through his hair, holding him to her breast as he sucked her, the sensation going deep between her thighs.

"You like that?"

"Yes," she said. "Basically, whatever you do, assume I like it." Her voice sounded desperate. Panting. She loved every minute of the moment. Of his touch.

He moved his hands up then, cupped her breasts as he took his attention back to her mouth. As he kissed her, deep and thorough while his thumbs skimmed over her breasts.

"Please," she begged.

He unsnapped her jeans, undid the zipper, and she began to kick her shoes off while he pushed her pants and underwear down her legs.

And then she was just naked. In front of him. In front of Jace. And it felt right. It felt good.

The way that he looked at her... Like he wanted to devour her. And she was ready. Ready for it to be more than just a dangerous glint in his eye, a hint, a promise. She was ready for it to be real.

He put his hands around her waist, smoothed them down her hips and back up, skimming the undersides of her breasts, before traversing a path down her body again, and all the while, his eyes were locked onto hers. His gaze intense. She shivered, and she wanted to look away, but she found that she couldn't. All she could do was stand there, trembling beneath his hands.

"So beautiful," he said.

And then he picked her up, like she weighed nothing, held her in his arms as he carried her to her bedroom. Of course he knew exactly where it was. He had been in it any number of times, but not with these dangerous eyes. Not with her naked and him halfway there.

But that he knew where he was spoke again to the familiarity of what they were.

He set her down at the center of the bed and

stood back, kicking his boots off, his hands going to his belt.

And she froze. She wanted to see him. Jace. She had never seen him naked. Of course she hadn't. She had never seen a naked man before. She could see the outline of his arousal through the faded denim of his jeans.

He was big. Not that she had any comparison or anything like that. But she could still tell he was big.

She licked her lips as he began to undo the belt buckle. As he began to pull the leather and slide it through the belt loops slowly.

"Yes," she whispered.

"You looking forward to this?" he asked, his voice husky.

"Yes," she confirmed, her own voice sounding scratchy.

"Good. Because it's for you, baby. This is definitely for you."

"Don't call me that," she said.

"Don't call you what?"

"Don't call me 'baby,' please. Call me Cara."

"Cara," he said, his voice coming out a growl.

He pushed his jeans and underwear off and revealed the extent of his arousal.

"Oh my," she said.

"Now that's not like you at all," he said.

He was confident, no nerves at all, and he didn't

need them. He was gorgeous. Every inch of him sculpted and lean and glorious.

His manhood was thick and just plain beautiful. She wouldn't have expected she'd think that about male anatomy, but she damn sure did. About Jace.

He moved over to the bed and pushed one knee down into the mattress, looking at her. Then he put his hands on her knees, smoothed them up her thighs, before forcing her legs apart.

"Jace," she said, the word a protest.

"Don't hide from me," he said, the command so firm she had no choice but to obey. She relaxed her thighs, let her legs fall open.

"That's right," he said. "Show me everything, baby. Show me."

She relaxed even further, and she felt herself getting more and more aroused beneath the sharpness of his gaze. Then he pushed his fingers right between her slick folds, finding her wet with desire for him.

Heat flared in his eyes. "You're so perfect, Cara. So perfect. And I need to taste you now."

She was about to protest, she really was, but then he lowered his head, buried his face between her thighs, and his tongue was so perfect and unerring that she couldn't breathe. Couldn't think.

She looked down, and immediately, her arousal inched its way up higher. Impossibly so. But it was undeniably Jace's head there. Between her legs. Undeniably her best friend licking her, tasting her.

She gasped, the beginnings of her orgasm pulsing from deep within her. And then he pushed a finger inside of her, and she lost it completely. She pulsed around him, arching her hips upward as her release slammed into her.

"You're so hot," he growled, moving up her body and capturing her mouth with a kiss. She could taste her own desire on his lips, and she found herself right back where she had been only moments ago. Turned on and ready to go.

He kissed her as he worked a second finger inside of her, and she moaned, letting her head relax against the pillow. There was so much that she wanted to do. She wanted to pleasure him with her mouth. She wanted to kiss him all over. She wanted… Him. All of him. But she didn't have the words to say that, because she was simply lost. Lost in the moment, lost in him.

He pushed a third finger inside of her and she arched her hips into the stinging discomfort.

"I know you said you had a vibrator. But I still want to make sure you're ready."

"Believe me," she whispered. "I'm ready."

And it was absurd. These impossibly intimate things they were doing. That they could go from being platonic all their whole relationship, to this, in the space of only an hour didn't seem real.

And somehow it seemed right all the same.

Because it had been there. Beneath the surface.

Because it wasn't random. Because it hadn't come from nothing. Because it was the truth, was the thing. The truth of how she felt about him.

And she supposed the truth of how he felt about her, even if it was limited to the physical and didn't extend to anything emotional.

Because you couldn't take this. Couldn't manufacture it, and she wasn't even tempted to ask if he was just doing her a favor. Because he was different in this moment. Because it wasn't brotherly Jace who had helped her out of any number of scrapes or taught her how to shoot or anything like that.

She would know if that's what he was doing, because she knew him.

"I hope you have… Condoms," she said.

"Yeah. I do."

The words were strange, the tendons in his neck standing out.

He withdrew from her and went to where he had discarded his jeans, grabbed his wallet and took out a condom packet. He tore it open, then positioned the protection over the head of his arousal, rolling it down slowly, gritting his teeth as he did. It was so erotic to see that. She shivered. And her teeth were still chattering when he came back to the bed, when he steadied her with a kiss, settling between her thighs, and the blunt head of his arousal pressed against the soft, slick entrance of her body, and she held her breath as he filled her.

Yeah, she had penetrated herself with a vibrator before. But that was different. It was hard, and it hadn't been this big.

She could feel him, pulsing inside of her. She could feel how this was different.

And it was... Him.

She looked up at him, and their eyes met. She fought against a strange swell of emotion in her chest. Jace. Jace was inside of her, and she didn't think anything could have prepared her for that. For the enormity of it. For what it meant. And suddenly, it did feel like too much. It felt like too much too fast. Too much for forever. Because one thing she couldn't deny was how deep her feelings ran for him when he pushed himself all the way inside of her and she felt whole. Complete. Felt like she had never wanted anything quite so badly.

Jace.

She didn't know if she said it out loud, screamed it, whispered it, or if it just resonated in her soul. All she knew was that he was there. And she wanted him.

All she knew was that it was too late to turn away. All she knew was that there would be no going back to the way things were before. Because it was too profound. Too real. Too utterly and completely earth-shattering.

And then he began to move, and each thrust of his body within hers pushed her closer and closer to that inevitable peak. She would've thought that it had been too much. Too intense that last time for her to be able to achieve it again, but here she was. His movements became sharp, hard. And that was when it was like being lit on fire. When there was no more control. No more tenderness because he was trying to take her innocence into account. This was hard and rough and primal. It was what she had asked for. She wrapped her legs around his waist, and it made him go deeper. She gasped at the impossibility of it. And how glorious it was.

"Jace..."

"Cara," he ground out, thrusting hard and fast until his control unraveled completely. Until it was like a desperate race to the finish line. She screamed out her pleasure before she even realized her orgasm had crashed over her. And then she was lost. Swept out to sea. Couldn't find a foothold. Couldn't get purchase.

"Jace." She said his name again. It was her battle cry. Her prayer. Her sanctuary and her tempest all at once.

And then his own release took him. He lowered his head, pressing his forehead hard against hers and pumping into her wildly, before going still, and she could feel him pulse deep inside of her. He growled, something feral and uncivilized as his release took hold. And then they lay there together. Sweat slicked and breathing hard.

And she tried to remember the before moment.

When they had been the way they'd always been. When they hadn't seen each other naked. When he hadn't been inside of her. And she realized that moment would never be able to stand on its own ever again.

Because they would've always done this.

Because every memory she had of him now would be colored with knowledge.

Of who he was when he made love. What he looked like beneath his clothes. How it felt to have him buried deep within her.

It wasn't just the after that was changed. It was the before.

And she really hadn't taken that into account. But here they were. Inglorious and changed.

Reduced to the very essence of who human beings ever were. Horny, sweaty messes, who had reveled in improbable things only a moment before.

And there was not another person in the world she could have ever done it with. She knew that much. It was clear as could be.

She didn't want him to say anything. Because she didn't want to move from this space into the next one. She didn't think she could handle it. She just needed to sit in the quiet for another second, try to find her breath.

She wasn't sure that was possible. So she just kept

on trying until her eyelids got heavy, and the last thing she saw before she drifted off to sleep was him lying beside her.

Nine

He couldn't remember the last time he'd had a cigarette, but thankfully, along with condoms, they were always in his pocket.

Because sometimes, after a night of heavy drinking, only a little nicotine would do. He hadn't been drunk on alcohol tonight, though. It was her.

The night was still and cold, and he sat out there on her back porch, staring off into the darkness. He didn't have his truck, so he couldn't leave. Anyway, leaving after he had just…

After he'd just screwed his best friend's brains out, was maybe not the best way to go. But then, was he screwing her brains out, or had she done it to him? It was hard to say.

It never felt anything like that before. Their connection, combined with the chemistry... It was unreal.

He flicked the switch on the lighter until it started up, lit the cigarette and took a deep drag off of it, then watched the glowing red end and the smoke curl up into the night.

"What are you doing out there?"

He turned around and saw Cara looking at him through her partially opened window.

"Sorry. Didn't realize the window was open."

"I woke up before I smelled the cigarette smoke."

She shut the window, and a moment later, the glass door slid open, and she stepped outside. "What's this?"

"Nothing. Just... Cigarette break."

"You don't smoke."

"Not usually. But, sometimes."

"Is this when I find out a whole bunch of things about you I didn't know?"

"It wasn't a secret."

"I guess."

She sat in the chair next to him. There was the space of a small, round table between them. She was dressed in an oversize T-shirt and nothing more. Her blond hair was a wreck. And he knew why.

A knot of guilt formed in his chest.

Was it guilt? He didn't think it was. It was something else entirely.

He wanted to call it uncertainty. But the fact of the matter was… It was a resistance of certainty.

He'd taken care of her. It was what he had purposed to do. He had a great time having sex with her. It had been great. They'd both enjoyed it. So there was nothing to feel guilty about. She'd consented enthusiastically, as had he.

It was what he felt like required doing in the aftermath.

"So why don't you tell me why you've never been with anybody before."

"Really?"

"Well. I have licked you between your legs, Cara Summers. So I think that maybe we don't need to have barriers up between us."

"Tell me about the cigarette, first."

"Sometimes I smoke after sex. There. It's that basic. Or when I'm really drunk. Sometimes both of those things are happening at the same time."

"Oh. It's just…"

"It's relaxing," he said. "That's all."

"I see."

And hell, because he had had his face between her legs, he didn't really see the point in holding back the truth of it. "I was never really all that into hard drugs. And let me tell you, there's opportunity for all of that out on the rodeo. I've tried just about everything. But mostly, what I learned was how to smooth out the rough edges incrementally. Little whiskey here and there, an orgasm is a great sleeping pill. A cigarette will finish you off. That's it. When I don't want to think anymore, those are the things that I do. I'm a high-functioning self-medicator."

"Oh. I guess I just… I see you as someone who's amazing and strong and doing really well. I guess sometimes I don't see how much pain you're still in."

"No, didn't you hear what I just said? I'm not in pain, because I know how to keep all that going. An unbroken chain."

"Sure. So it's not really because of me specifically. This is just a thing you do."

"I needed to think."

"Did you… I mean… Was the sex good for you?"

He sat up straight. "You can be in any doubt of that?"

"Yes. I can. Because I'm just a person. A person who is very… Vulnerable, when it comes right down to it. There's a reason that I haven't been with any-body. And that is what you wanted to know. I grew up so isolated in a lot of ways. Everybody here was mean to me. I wasn't cool. I was this poor, very un-fashionable girl, who lived with her grandpa. White trash. My mom was a drug addict and everybody knew it. And I never knew who my dad was, and everybody knew that too. I was one of those kids. The ones that nobody wanted to touch. And it was my grandpa, and the bar and the town that ended up grounding me here. And yeah, I like to flirt at the bar. But can you imagine if I actually let any one of those guys sleep with me? Then they would all think that they could. It's all fun and games when it's flirting." She looked away. "And anyway, what I said is true. I saw you touch this woman one time... All I could think about was what that must be like. And I swear to you, Jace, you are my friend, and you always have been. And I feel guilty about this. I do. But I've thought about sleeping with you. A lot."

He took another drag on the cigarette. "Tell me," he said, blowing the smoke out into the air.

"The night before the hotel... The night before I... I told you that I was a virgin... I couldn't sleep. I started thinking about you and... Then it seemed like the easiest thing in the world to touch myself."

He flicked the cigarette down onto the ground and twisted his boot over the top of it. "What are you telling me exactly?"

"I touch myself sometimes and think about you. About you being the one to touch me. About us... In bed together."

"You know, it's a good thing I never knew about that before now. Because you would not have been untouched all this time."

"You don't feel violated by that?"

"Did you really think I would?"

"I don't know. Sometimes I felt really guilty about it. Like it was an invasion of your privacy. But..."

"But, you were too horny to care?"

She laughed, and he could see that her cheeks had been stained dark pink with just a little bit of charming embarrassment. "I guess. Isn't that kind of the human condition?"

"Yeah. Often. I guess tonight is a good example of that. Look, Cara, for me… I decided a long time ago that I wasn't going to look at you that way. I wasn't going to let myself think about you that way because I had to protect you. For all the people that were mean to you, from anything that they might say. Because you're right. There was stuff. About your parents. And I didn't want anybody to think that I was using you like that, and say the kinds of things about you that they said about your mom."

"Oh."

"So that's one reason. The other is just that I wanted to take care of you the way that I would've taken care of Sophia. And so I put you hard in that category. Sister. I wanted to treat you like my sister. But you weren't my sister. That's the thing. And it's funny, because I fancy myself a realist. I don't talk to ash bottles on the shelf in the back of a bar. But I sure as hell have spent my life trying to compensate for her not being here like she could see it. Like she can see what I'm doing. Like it might mean something to her. Shit. I never really realized that about myself. It's a hell of a thing. It really is. I like to tell myself that I'm too… Logical. Realistic. But I'm just

living as a tribute for a ghost I claim I don't even believe in. So, what am I supposed to do with that?"

"But not tonight," she said softly, looking down
at her hands.

"No. Not tonight. That was about you and me."

And yet again, that feeling rose up inside of his
chest. That booming need to do something.

He'd been telling himself that he didn't know what
he wanted for the last couple of months, and yet at
the end of the day, he was pretty sure he knew what
he had to do.

"Will you come back to bed?"

"Yeah," he said. "Just a minute."

"Will you brush your teeth first?"

"Only because you asked nicely," he said.

She stood up, and walked back toward the house
and turned and looked at him just one last time before she slipped into the glass door.

And he sat out there for just a few moments longer, until everything inside of him went still. Until
all his certainty crystallized.

Then he stood up and went back toward her bedroom. But not before he stopped and brushed his
teeth.

He had kissed her goodbye this morning around
five o'clock, and she had a feeling that had been on
purpose, because they hadn't had a chance to talk.

The kiss hadn't been on her mouth. It had just been on her cheek.

They hadn't had sex again. He pulled her up against him and said something about her being sore, and told her to go to sleep. She didn't know how she got home—if he called one of his brothers or if he'd taken a cab...

She felt a little bit melancholy, and she carried that all through her day. Her offer was accepted on the hotel, and she made an appointment to go and sign papers. It also happened to work out that the contractor she wanted to use was free to meet with her at the property that afternoon. And all of that should've been great and exciting and more than enough of a distraction to stop thinking about Jace.

It was perfectly normal for them to not have communicated on a random Thursday.

It was just that they had never not communicated on a random Thursday the night after they'd had sex.

They'd had sex.

She wasn't a virgin anymore.

Sex sounded so clinical, even in her head.

She would call it making love, but it hadn't been especially sweet either. It had been... Wrenching. A rending.

It had been something else entirely.

And now so was she. And maybe so were they.

She couldn't shake that image of him, sitting with his elbows on his knees in that chair on her back patio, the cigarette between his fingers. His cowboy hat on like he was fixing to leave in the middle of the night.

She had to say something to him. Because he was her friend.

Because she didn't want him to go.

She sighed and pulled her truck up to the front of the hotel. It was almost hers. Just a few signature pages away.

The contractor was already there, his big white truck parked out front. She got out and tried to smile. She'd been trying to smile all day.

"Hey," she said. "Glad you could make it by today."

"Good to see you, Cara."

Mike Colton was a regular at the bar, and they had a pretty good rapport. He was never flirtatious and didn't flirt with any other women in the bar, which was good, considering he was married. So she had a pretty high opinion of him right off the bat. Plus, she knew he did good work.

"Let's take a walk through the place."

She heard the sound of an engine, and turned around. Just as Jace pulled right into the driveway.

"Oh," she said.

Her mind went blank. Jace put the truck in Park and got out, and her tongue was suddenly as dry as a patch of scrub brush. "I didn't... I didn't realize that you were coming," she said.

"Of course. I just figured… You know, it's my investment. I thought I'd come by and look."

Except he hadn't known that she was meeting with the contractor today, because they hadn't talked. So she wondered what had really compelled him to come by here.

Yeah. She really did.

"Good to have you," said Mike. Who, to his credit, did not immediately start deferring to Jace, which made her feel even better about choosing him to be the contractor.

Except suddenly she was resentful. Resentful that she was in the middle of the contractor meeting. Because she wondered why Jace had come to find her. She wondered why he was really here. And she wondered what he was thinking.

She went around to the back, where the lockbox was, and popped it open, taking the key out from the inside. "Here," she said. "I'll show you the inside."

They walked in, and Mike started explaining about the good bones and all kinds of other things that construction types said.

"It's nice," she said. "It just needs some updating."

"Yeah. If you don't mind, I'll take a walk through, and I'll let you know what I think."

"Yeah. Just, you let me know what you think homeowners are always asking you for. I need to make sure that I have all the amenities that I could possibly want for guests."

"I'm betting it's going to focus a lot on the bathrooms," he said. "That can get expensive. But believe me, it's always worth the investment."

"She can afford it," said Jace.

Mike smiled, then started to walk through the room, clipboard in hand, making notes.

She turned to face Jace, the minute they were alone. "How did you know that I would be here?"

"I didn't. I happened to be driving to the bar. I saw your truck parked out front."

"Oh."

"I was looking for you."

"You were?"

"Yeah. I wanted to talk to you. Because…" He stopped talking. He wrapped his arm around her waist and pulled her up against his body, full-length, and then he kissed her. Kissed her the way she wished he would've done this morning. Kissed her the way she wanted so desperately to be kissed.

"Oh," she breathed.

"Cara…"

"Sorry," said Mike, clearing his throat. "I just wanted to show you something concerning."

"It's already concerning," said Jace.

"Is it a hole where raccoons could get in?" Cara asked.

Mike frowned. "No. Am I looking for one of those?"

"Yes," said Jace and Cara at the same time.

Mike's eyebrows shot up. "Look, as long as you're realistic about the place."

"I think we're pretty realistic," she said.

Mike led them back to the pantry area where there was some rotted wood in the back. "I'm just worried I'm going to find more things like this," said Mike.

"Like I said," Jace said. "We really do have the budget. We don't want to cut any corners. This needs to be a luxury escape. Affordable, but the kind of people that want to travel here and stay in a historic place, want it to be charming without being uncomfortable. We don't want them thinking it just feels old and outdated. We definitely don't need soft floorboards."

"Of course not," she said.

Mike looked between the two of them, and she knew that they were now in an uphill battle with gossip. Because he had definitely seen them kiss.

"I'll keep looking around," said Mike.

"Well," she said, when they were alone in the pantry. "He saw that."

"Fine with me," said Jace.

"I mean, the argument could definitely be made that most people will think that we were already sleeping together, but…"

"I wanted to talk to you about that. I'm staying here. I'm not going back to the rodeo. I'm investing in the hotel. It isn't that I don't know what I want, it's that I was resisting what I want. You know I don't like dreams. And you know I like everything locked in place. I like it sure, I like it certain. The hotel's a little bit of a gamble, but I don't mind gambling with money. As for the rest… Nothing in my life is mine. And that's by design. Whatever I don't have, I don't have because I didn't want it. I love my family, but I recognized pretty early that loving people is painful. I've been riding the rodeo because it was there. Because it was something to do. But that's not enough for me anymore. I need something that's mine. I'm going to stay in Lone Rock—that's what I'm trying to tell you."

Her heart started to throb. "And?"

"And I want you. I want you, Cara."

"You… You want me?"

It wasn't really a declaration of love… Did she even want a declaration of love? The very idea was sort of terrifying. She hadn't fully let herself process her feelings for him. And he was… Well, he wasn't a romantic. That much was sure and certain.

"Yes. I want…"

They heard footsteps again. "Hold that thought."

Mike returned. "Sorry," he said. "Just wanted you to look at some things in the bathroom."

"Rain check," he said.

Her heart was thundering so hard, she didn't think she could take a rain check. But they did decide that they would just go ahead and follow Mike while he looked around. "I'll write up a bid," he said an hour later. "One that's based primarily around modernizing the bathrooms, making sure you have new plumbing, good hot water heaters and modern fixtures in the kitchen, which I know won't really have anything to do with the guests, but if you're going to hire anybody to do some cooking… It'll make things easier."

She really didn't care about cooking. Or plumbing. Or anything but what Jace had been about to tell her, but she knew she couldn't completely abandon the point of all of this, not right now. Not when the point of this was business, and not for her to kiss Jace. But she really wanted to kiss Jace.

And find out exactly what he had been about to tell her.

"It all sounds great," she said. "Thanks, Mike."

And she smiled, hoping that he would get the idea that her smile was the period at the end of this sentence. And he did, giving them a half wave and heading out the door.

She looked up at Jace. "I would really like to hear what you were going to tell me."

"Well. You're my best friend. And I want to be part of this venture with you… And you know, I just don't like halfway shit. I think we should get married."

Ten

He'd thought about it. He was confident in it. And he knew that there were a whole lot of people who wouldn't understand how he had gone from friends, to sex once, to wanting to get married, but he wasn't a man who operated in halfway zones. He was a man of absolutes. He hadn't committed to anything, not for all of his life. And if he was going to commit to any one thing, then it was going to be Cara. There was no way he was going to have sex with her, then pretend that it hadn't happened. There was no way that he was going to…

No. There was no way on earth that he was going to be cool with her moving on and being with other people. And that meant that there was only one option available to him. Locking that shit down.

That was it.

He was in on the hotel. He was in on everything. Whatever she wanted, whatever she needed. He wanted to buy land. And he wanted to build a house on it. And he was going to... He was going to do what he had always promised that he would do. He was going to take care of this woman.

That feels perilously close to a dream.

It wasn't a dream. It was action. It was a plan. It was what needed to happen.

"I... I don't understand."

"The way I see it, it's about the only option we have. Do you want me to sleep with someone else?"

"Hell no," she said.

"I don't want you to sleep with anyone else. Do you want to sleep together a couple more times and see where it goes, take the chance that it might burn out?"

"I..."

"No. Because do you think we can possibly go back? Do you think that we can pretend that never happened?"

"No. And it's why it never did before. And it's why it was... Well, I guess it was a bad idea."

"But it wasn't an idea, was it? It was a thing, and it happened. And I think it was undeniable. Neither of us decided to do it. We didn't just think... Well let's see what happens. We didn't think at all. And listen, when it comes to life, one thing I know is that I'm committed to you. I'm committed to you in a way that

I never have been to anyone I'm not related to. So one thing I know for sure is that I've always wanted you to be in my life for all my life. I was never planning on having it be any different. So if I'm going to put down roots, those roots are going to tangle up with yours, Cara. That's just a fact."

"I don't know what to say, Jace. I… I really didn't expect for you to be proposing after one time of being together."

"Think about it. How would it have ever ended in another way?"

It couldn't. That was the thing. And yes, they were different. She was sparkly and fantastical, and he was him. But there had never been another person that he had ever known needed to be by his side for the rest of forever.

"The thing is," said Cara. "You usually travel for half the year. And… You're one of my favorite people on earth. Hell, I think you might be my favorite person on earth, but living together and… And we had sex once."

"What do you want from your life? I mean, do you want to work at the bar every night until two thirty in the morning?"

"No. It's why I'm expanding. It's why I'm buying the hotel."

"Did you want to get married? Start a family?"

"Do you?"

It was a good question, because he'd never given

much thought to it. It was part and parcel of the whole not thinking ahead thing. "If you want kids, then yeah."

He would give her whatever she wanted. He realized that. Whatever was in his power to give, he was going to. Because she was Cara, and she had been essential to him from the time they were kids. And he never dreamed of a wife and a family, but... He'd have kids. For her.

"But you don't want them."

"No. I think you're misunderstanding. It doesn't matter what I want. Or maybe better put, what I want is tangled up with what you want. With what makes you happy." What he knew, the conclusion he'd come to, after he'd gotten up at the butt crack of dawn and gone out to work himself to death, because it was the only way to get any kind of mental clarity was that he couldn't imagine letting another man take that position in her life. It wouldn't do. There would be no burning out his attraction for her. There would be no forgetting that those things had passed between them.

And that meant making it permanent. Whatever that looked like for her.

He had done his level best to be whatever she needed over all these years, and he would keep on doing it.

"Can I... Take a rain check on that question?"

"You're the one who asked it."

"Yeah. Kind of. I asked what you wanted, and...

Never mind." He could see that something was bothering her.

"I want this," he said, something intense tugging at his chest. Undeniable. "Because there's no other way that I can imagine us getting all the things that we want. You and me. Together. And together like we were last night."

"I… You know, half of what bothers me about this is everybody's just going to think they were right all along."

He couldn't help it. He laughed. Because of course of all the things that would bother Cara, what other people thought—not in terms of appearances, but just in terms of her being proved wrong in any kind of way—was high on her list.

"Yeah. We are going to get mercilessly harassed by my brothers."

"I'm not sure anything is worth it," said Cara.

"You know it is," he said. "Come on. Remember last night?"

And she turned pink. From the roots of her blond hair, all the way down to her breasts. At least, the part that he could see.

"Cara. Don't you want that?"

"Yes," she whispered. "I do. But marriage is a big step and I just don't…"

"Remember what I said, about the ride. About the certainty. I don't do halfway. I don't and I won't. The only reason that I felt uncertain these last few months is because I knew I needed to make a decision. It was either go back all the way, or be here all the way. I felt all this time like I didn't have anything that was mine. Like I didn't have anything to claim. While I do now."

"Are you… Claiming me?"

"Yes. I sure as hell am claiming you. As mine. My best friend. My lover. I hope my wife."

"It's just… It's a lot. And it's like a complete one-eighty from where we were just a couple of days ago? I don't…"

"It's not a one-eighty. It was just a step closer to each other. There's not another person that I can think about living in a house with. Building a life with. You know, it really pains me to say that Boone was right. We're in each other's lives, and now we're in business together. We are enmeshed in each other's lives in every single way. It feels right. It feels like time."

And he had never meant anything half so much as he meant this.

"You're really not going to let me even think about this?"

"Do you need to?"

Her eyebrows shot up. "You really are kind of an arrogant son of a bitch."

"Yeah, but you knew that about me. You knew that the whole time."

"I did, but I guess I've never been in a position where it was directed at me."

"Oh it has. It's just that I dial it up in increments, and eventually, you get kind of dead to it."

She laughed. "Apparently not."

He leaned in, and right then, he couldn't take it anymore. He wanted her. He needed her. He hadn't realized how much until he had showed up at the house and seen her.

That was the thing—this wasn't going away. And he was a man who made decisions. A man who went with the moment.

And the moment had dictated that they kiss. It had demanded that they go to bed together. And that turn of events demanded this. And nothing less.

That was the simple truth of it all. And so he kissed her. On an indrawn breath. Captured it with his lips and turned it into a sigh of desire.

"Please," he said.

"Oh shit. Now you even said please? That really is a miracle."

He smiled against her mouth, and he felt her smile back.

He kissed her, and he was overwhelmed by the reality of it all. That it was her.

And the rightness of it too. Now that he'd made the decision… It was right. It was just right.

The decisiveness roared through him. And suddenly, it was like every piece of his life was locked into place, in perfect alignment. For the first time in maybe ever.

This was right. This was what he was supposed to be, where he was supposed to be, with who he was supposed to be with.

So he kissed her. Right there in the ghost hotel, right there, where all this had started. Or maybe it had started long before. Before she had ever looked up at him with those starry green eyes and told him that she was still a virgin.

She wasn't anymore. He'd seen to that. Now she was his.

He picked her up, because he liked to do that, and carried her toward the stairs. She wrapped her arms around his neck and kept on kissing him, and they went down the hall, to that room, where they had shared a bed, because this time, he aimed to share it with her properly.

The curtains were still drawn around it, and he pushed them aside and set her down on the blankets.

"You know," she said. "None of it's actually dusty."

"You know, I wouldn't have cared if it was. Because all I can think about is being inside of you again."

"I might've thought about the dust. But I appreciate that as a ringing endorsement of my sexual prowess."

"You wouldn't have been thinking about dust." He kissed her lips, her cheek, her neck. "I would've made sure of that."

He laid her back on the bed and let the curtain swing shut. It was dim behind the curtains, but he liked the intimacy that it gave. He stripped her shirt slowly from her body, and even in the dim light, he could see her shape just fine.

He unhooked her bra and threw it to the side. And he was in awe. Of the fact that he could do this with her now. That she was his, and he could just look his fill when he wanted to. No more restraint. No more pretending she wasn't the most beautiful woman he'd ever seen.

He moved to her jeans next, stripped her completely of her clothes and admired all of her. Her stomach, the curves, the dips, her belly button. That downy patch of pale curls at the apex of her thighs. Her legs.

All of her.

She had always been the strongest, funniest woman he'd ever known, and on some level, he'd known she was the sexiest, but he'd tried to keep himself from living in that space. And now he'd moved in permanently.

She was everything.

Absolutely everything.

He kissed her neck, her breasts. Kissed her until she was shivering. Teased them both.

And then suddenly, he felt her hand pressed against the center of his chest, pushing him away. She sat up, grabbing hold of the hem of his shirt and pulling it up over his head. It was like she had come alive with need. She explored his body, kissed his chest, went down his abs and started to undo his belt. And he knew where this was going next, and he did not have the fortitude to stop it. She unzipped his jeans and wrapped her hand around his arousal, exposing him. She pushed his pants and underwear down, and with her hand wrapped firmly around the base of him, leaned in and took him into her mouth.

"Shit," he said, grabbing hold of her ponytail and holding tight.

"I've never done this before," she said.

And hell. That just about took him out. Then and there.

It was nearly over before it started.

"Damn, woman. You can't just say things like that."

"But I want you. I want this. I want you to know that you're the only one. I want you, with all your marriage proposal, and your certainty to know, that you're the man I fantasized about. You're the man that I wanted. You're the only man I wanted to lick like this." And she made direct eye contact with him while she slid her tongue from the base of his shaft all the way to the tip. "You're the only one I ever wanted to take in deep."

And that was exactly what she did next. And all he could do was hang on. Let her pleasure him. Let her make him his. He wanted her. He wanted this. This was her staking her claim. His had been a marriage proposal, while she was branding him with his own desire. Letting him know that he would never, ever own his own need again. Because it would always be in the palms of Cara Summers's hands.

He let her pleasure him like that until it became too much. Until he got too close to the edge.

"Come on," he said, his voice rough. "I want to be inside you."

"You were inside me," she said, a little grin tugging at the corners of her mouth.

"You know what I mean."

"No, I don't. You're gonna have to tell me."

"I want inside where you're all wet for me. Just for me. You saved that for me too, didn't you?"

And he would never see anything half so beautiful as his best friend blushing over his dirty talk for her.

And if that was his future, and if that was marriage, it made him want to look forward to it just a little bit.

But there was no need to look forward. Because they could just exist in these moments. Every day until the wedding. Because she would say yes. Of course she would. Because how could they ever go back. Which meant it had to be always. They couldn't take a chance on anything else.

He took his wallet out of his back pocket and took a new condom out of there, then kicked his jeans and shoes off the rest of the way, before rolling the protection on quickly. Then he rolled over onto his back, gripped her hips and brought her down over him. "Next lesson. I want you to ride me. So that I can watch you. Give me a show."

He brought her down slowly, positioning her on his aching length. She moaned, grabbing hold of his shoulders as she flexed her hips, taking him in deep. She began to move her hips, gracefully, elegantly. Like dirty poetry. And he had always imagined that his own brand of hedonism and Cara's divinity could never mix, but he was being proven wrong here and now. Because something he would've said was profane, was very definitely not, not here and now. It felt sanctified somehow, and he would never be able to explain that.

And when she reached up and cupped her own breast, squeezed herself, then her nipple, as she continued to flex her hips over him, he just about died, and he'd be hard-pressed to deny the fact that he saw God in that moment.

Her golden hair was wild, and her lips were parted, her eyes closed. As she moved over him, riding them both into a frenzy.

And finally, he lost his patience. He turned her over onto her back, pinning her to the mattress, his thrusts hard and deep. She moaned, arching up against him off the mattress, and her orgasm broke over her, squeezing him tight. "Jace," she said. And when she said his name it was music. When she said his name, it was fuel to the fire.

When she said his name, it was everything.

But it was when she bit her lip and looked up at him, those green eyes staring straight into him, as if she could see all the way down into what he was, that was when he lost it. It was when he looked full in the face of his best friend in all the world, while the wet clasp of her body was tight around his arousal, while her breasts were pressed up against his chest—that was when he lost it.

His orgasm was merciless, grabbing him by the throat and all but tearing it out, the growl that rose up from inside of him a prayer and a curse all in one.

And this seemed right. Sealing their new life together in this place. This place that had triggered it. This place that had been the first step.

He held her close on the bed for a long moment, until their heartbeats calmed down.

"Yes," she said softly. "Yes, Jace, I'll marry you."

"Good," he said, dropping a kiss on the top of her head. Because he could do that now. Because he could kiss her and touch her, and she could do the same to him, because they had erased those barriers between them. And he meant it, that it was good, but he couldn't help but wonder if he'd said the wrong thing, because she didn't look joyously happy, but she buried her face against his shoulder and fell asleep, so he figured it wasn't all bad either.

How could it be?

They were best friends.

Eleven

She really wished that she had a different friend, other than Jace. And she had never really wished that before. She was perfectly fine having all of her friendship eggs in one basket. But the problem was, she had her friendship eggs in his basket, and now her relationship eggs, and she just wished that there was somebody that she could talk to. Somebody that would be able to reassure her that she was making the right choice. It was just that… Jace hadn't said anything about being in love with her. And it was because she knew he wasn't.

The thing with Jace was he was hardheaded, and he was stubborn. And he damn sure thought that his way was the best way. But what she couldn't figure out was exactly why he had decided that he wanted this. She could circle around it. But she didn't think she was quite hitting his motivation on the head, and that worried her a little bit. That she couldn't quite parse it. Yes, she understood that he wanted to put down roots.

Yes, she understood that he could only see this going one of two ways.

That they would eventually take other lovers, or they had to commit to each other. And since Jace was kind of a paperwork, lock, stock, and barrel kind of guy, for him, the answer would be marriage, and not just moving in together. She knew him well enough to understand all of that. But she felt like there was something deeper. And the problem with Jace was he would never admit to that. He would never admit to the deeper. He would never even say it to himself. He was the man who swore up and down there was nothing after this life and he was totally fine with it. He was the man who didn't believe in manifesting your dreams or any of that.

And she was the one who still talked to her grandpa like he was right there with her.

A slight smile lifted the corner of her mouth, and she turned and looked up at the Jack Daniel's bottle. "Well. Jace wants me to marry him. I don't know if you already know that. I kind of hope that you haven't been spying on us. All things considered. But I told him yes and I'm worried. I'm kind of in love with him. Or I'm really in love with him. And I don't think that that's part of this for him. And that scares me."

She waited. For something. For a rush of wisdom. A glowing butterfly.

She didn't get any of it.

"I think that if I told Jace I loved him he would run away. Because it's like… He wants to do all these external things to take control, but it's the stuff that he can't control that he can't deal with. And I get it. It's because of Sophia."

She took a deep breath. She wasn't getting any answers. Not out of the silent whiskey bottle.

There was a knock at the back door of the bar, and she figured it was probably her delivery from the food services company. She went back into the kitchen, and opened the door. There was a stack of crates filled with various things. Frozen beef patties and other assorted things they needed for the kitchen. And then she heard a sound. A hawk. And she looked up, and saw a bird circling. And it filled her with a strange sort of hope. Sort of resolve.

"Is that you, Grandpa?"

And then it was like she could see his face.

I'm dead. I got better things to do than hang around here.

That's what he would say. And it made her laugh.

Well, maybe that was her answer. Her grandpa had better things to do than hang around here, so maybe she needed to get her life in order. Buy the hotel. Marry Jace. She didn't want anything else. She didn't want anyone else. She wasn't losing anything by marrying him. Yes, the emotions would always be tricky with him. But he cared about her. And it wasn't like she had another man who was desperately in love with her waiting in the wings. It was just... It was just knowing that she maybe cared a little bit more than he did. That was the tough thing. But it would be worth it. It would be worth it to be with him.

Her phone buzzed.

She looked down at the text that she had just gotten.

Dinner with my family tonight?

And she knew that her answer would cement this forever.

Yes.

Yes. She was going to marry Jace. And his family was going to say I told you so, and it would be totally worth it.

Twelve

It was handy that his sister Callie and her husband, Jake, had been planning on coming to spend a few days anyway. They would be here for the announcement, and that meant that he only had to tell everyone in his family one time what he was going to do. That he was leaving the rodeo, that he was getting married. All of that suited him. It suited him right down to the very ground his boots were standing on.

He had it all mapped out in his mind. Yeah, there might've been some merit to giving his mother at least a warning prior to making the announcement, but he just didn't want to get into it. He only wanted to do it once, and he wanted Cara to be there when he did. Because it would make them behave. Maybe.

He had also spent part of the day looking at land. He wanted something that was near enough to town that it would be easy for Cara to manage her interests right there on Main Street, but far enough out that they had a good-size plot of land, and opportunity to make it functional.

He was still deciding what exactly he wanted to ranch. Bison, beef or horses. All completely different endeavors.

Roots.

That's what he was doing now. It was the thing he was doing.

What he didn't anticipate, was how Cara would look when she showed up.

He was in his truck, out in front of his parents' palatial country home, all square lines and lots of glass, when Cara rolled up.

He had seen her in a lot of different things. She typically wore blue jeans. She liked her rhinestones, did his girl, and on the evenings that she worked at the bar, she favored a scoop neck, tight tank top all the better to show off her figure. He was used to her in all these things. The casual T-shirt Cara, and sexy nighttime Cara.

But when she got out of the truck and revealed that she was in a soft, floaty sundress, it just about did him in. It had little short sleeves and a rounded neck with a little bow right at the center of her breasts that he desperately wanted to undo immediately. It was short, coming inches above her knees, swinging when she walked. Her blond hair was loose, curling at the ends and blowing in the breeze, and he was suddenly desperate to touch it.

What was this? This shift.

Because somehow, in that moment, it wasn't about being attracted to his friend. It felt bigger somehow. It wasn't just about having permission to find her beautiful—it was about this woman, this relationship, and something deepening.

He had thought of it as adding something on. But now it seemed like it was just all that they had been, but deeper.

"Look at you," he said.

As he got closer, he could see that she had painted her lips with something glossy and nice, that she had just a little bit of mascara and some gold and green eye shadow that highlighted her eyes.

She was sexy and sweet, exactly how you would want a woman to look that you were bringing home to meet your parents and tell them you were going to marry her.

Of course, she had met his parents before.

So it was more about presenting her as his future wife, rather than his friend.

Except when he reached out and took her hand in his, she was still his friend. And when he leaned in and kissed her lips, she was still his friend. And something expanded in his chest all the same.

They walked up the steps together, hand in hand.

"If we walk in like this they're going to know."

"Yeah. I'm committed to presenting this as if it's a thing they should all be aware of."

She laughed. "Okay. I'm sure Flint and Boone won't give you a hard time in that case."

"As long as you stop flirting with them."

"Probably I won't," she said. "Because it bugs you."

And it was his turn to laugh, because she was so committed to being her, and it was one of the things he liked the very most about her.

That she was cantankerous and stubborn and every inch herself. That she wasn't going to change or become softer or bend just because they were sleeping together. Just because she'd agreed to marry him.

"Yeah, well. I might put my foot down about the men at the bar," he said. Because he was testing her. Because he couldn't help himself.

"You're going to put your foot down?"

"I said what I said."

A little smile tugged at the corner of her mouth. "Jace Carson, have we met?"

"Yes we have. Intimately. Naked."

She shoved him against his shoulder. "Sometimes I think you're still the same boy from when we were twelve."

"Close enough."

Except he didn't feel like that boy. He wasn't sure what he felt like. Resolved, so there was that.

He opened up the front door into the house so

that she didn't knock—and they walked inside. His whole family was sitting in the broad, expansive living room, on the different couches and chairs in front of the floor to ceiling windows that overlooked the brilliant view. They were missing Buck, who could come back but wouldn't. And Sophia, who was simply gone. And it pained him that those were the first things he thought of, seeing them all together. Just that they weren't all together. And probably never would be.

"Hey," he said. He grabbed hold of Cara's hand and led her into the room. He figured this was as good a time as any. "I'm glad everybody's here tonight."

"It's good to see you," said his sister Callie, popping up from her chair and reaching out to pull him into a hug. She was just a little bit pregnant, her belly starting to round out. He wondered if Sophia would've had kids by now, had she lived.

He wondered if he would have.

If his life would've been different.

If he could've believed in miracles of hope and love for longer.

But Cara felt like an anchor behind him, and he would take that instead.

"It's good to see everyone, but there's something that Cara and I want to tell you."

He looked over at his mother, who was looking at him with an expectation and joy he wondered how she still felt. His mother, who had always been so pretty and perfect. His mother, who had been devastated at Sophia's loss, but seemed to figure out how to keep on going once she had Callie. "We're getting married."

The roar that went through the room was massive.

"Pay up," said Chance.

"Fuck you," said Boone, reaching into his back pocket and pulling out his wallet.

"What?" he asked.

"We have had a bet going for a long time about whether or not you guys were really a couple," said Chance. "And I win. You owe me so much money. Brother, I know you don't have that kind of cash in your wallet, and you're gonna have to write me a check. But we're going to have to make sure that check is good."

"I have more money than you do," said Boone. "I have more endorsements. Because my face is prettier."

"Well, you owe money to me now."

"Are you kidding me?" he asked.

"Not at all," said Flint, shaking his head. "I didn't go in as hard as Chance did, but Boone owes me money too. But I figure if he wants to work it off…"

"I'm not doing your chores for you," said Boone angrily. He looked over at Jace. "You know, this should confirm that I'm your favorite brother," said Boone. "Because I believed you. You're a liar."

"What are the particulars of the bet?" Cara asked. She went and sat down on the chair facing his family. He supposed this was the very great perk of Cara knowing his family like she did. "Because, depending on if time lines and the like are part of the bet, you might actually not have won any money from Boone."

"Why?" asked Chance.

"Well, tell me the bet."

"That you been secretly sleeping together the whole time."

"Nope. You lose."

"Shit. Really?"

"Really."

"Well, I collect on the part where I said you would end up together."

"Yep," Cara said. "That you can have."

"When did you start sleeping together?" Chance asked. "Because that is probably something I can work out in terms of how much money I'm owed."

"Chance," said their mother, scolding. "Honestly."

"That's very crass," said Boone. "Why don't you just accept that you lost?"

"I didn't, though," said Chance. "Because they're getting married."

"Congratulations," said Kit. "Really."

"Yes," said his mother, standing up and coming over to them. She went to Cara first and took her hand. Cara stood, and something shifted inside of him as he watched his mother embrace Cara. "You're just perfect for him," she whispered. "Exactly what he needs."

That made something strange reverberate inside of his chest.

"Happy for you," his dad said, getting up from his chair and coming over to clap him on the back. "Damn thrilling to have four of you married. Growing the family like this. It's more than we could've ever hoped for."

"Dinner is ready," said his mother. As if she had cooked it. But then, what his mother was great at was catering. And he appreciated that. "Shall we go into the dining room?"

He walked over to where Cara was and took her hand, lingering in the living room for a moment as the rest of the family filtered in.

"You good?"

She looked up at him and she smiled, and that smile just about broke his heart. "Yes. I love your family. And the idea of actually being part of it is… It's amazing."

I love your family.

That did something to him. Echoed through his soul.

Dinner was a pretty damned beautiful roast duck and sides, and there was something about it that pulled him back to happier times with his family. It wasn't that they hadn't had happier times in the last few years—they had. But there was something that just felt bigger and more right. His sister being here with her husband. His brothers and their wives. Him and Cara. "I'm investing in the hotel. Cara just bought it," he said. "She's going to open it up and re-vamp it and bring more tourism into town."

"That's fantastic," said his sister-in-law Shelby.

"It'd be nice to get some of your beadwork to sell," said Cara. "And some art, maybe. I think it would be amazing to have work by indigenous artisans, so that people can get an idea of the real Lone Rock."

"Happy to oblige," said Shelby. "I love the idea of local art being featured."

"You can recommend anybody whose work you love locally."

"Now I'm drunk with power."

"Investing in business," said his dad. "That's un-like you."

"Well. I'm changing some things. I'm done with the rodeo."

His dad nodded slowly. "I thought you might be."

"Done with the rodeo and looking to buy land around here. So that Cara and I can build a house and start a family."

"I'm so happy for you," said Callie, beaming. "This is just great."

But for some reason, his family's joy wasn't quite touching him all the way down, and he couldn't for the life of him figure out why. Cara seemed happy, and he wanted more than anything for her to be happy. No question about that. None at all. He was doing all of the things that he had decided to, and he had announced it, he was certain.

He didn't know why uncertainty was following him. Because there really wasn't any reason for uncertainty. They finished up dinner, and Shelby and Cara had gotten involved in discussing logistics for selling art and featuring art throughout the hotel for sale, and he and his brothers took the opportunity to go into his parents' game room and throw some darts.

Usually, Callie would've joined the boys. But not today. Chance threw the first dart and hit the bull's-eye. The problem with this was they were all too good.

"Seriously, though," said Chance, when Kit's dart came from behind and hit his, knocking it out of position. "Congratulations. I'm glad that you finally opened your eyes to what you guys had this whole time."

"Same," said Kit.

Flint and Boone exchanged looks with each other. His brother-in-law, Jake, raised his glass of whiskey. "Absolutely. Marriage is the best damn thing."

"It is," Chance agreed.

"Spoken like a man who keeps his balls in his wife's purse," said Flint.

"Spoken like a man who has a diss track about

him that's currently number one on the country air-waves," Chance shot back.

"It is not a diss track. And it isn't about me."

"It's about you," said Boone.

"You're a turncoat," said Flint.

"The thing is," said Chance, "I think opening yourself up to all this… It's tough. It's tough to let go of all the shit that you've been through and decide that you want to… Hope."

"Don't go too far," said Jace, picking up a dart and flinging it at the dartboard. He missed the bull's-eye. What the hell was that about?

"It's not about hope or anything like that. It's just… It makes sense. I'm not gonna be in the rodeo forever. Not by a long shot. And I needed to decide what to do. I felt uncertain, but it was only because I was avoiding the most obvious thing. Clearly, going all in on being here is the answer. And then… Cara and I… You know, something happened."

"When exactly?" Chance asked.

"Not your business. But a couple of days ago."

"A couple of days ago?" Three of his brothers asked that at once.

"Yes," he said.

"And you just… Decided to marry her when the first time you've actually ever been with her was a couple of days ago?" Kit asked.

"Are you suggesting that I should be uncertain about what I want from her?"

"Not at all," said Kit. "I just thought maybe you guys were engaged in some kind of serious slow burn and you were just now ready to tell us all. I didn't know that it was like best friends, then you finally hooked up, and you're getting married right away. You didn't even have a chance to find out she's pregnant."

"We don't all have unprotected sex, Kit," said Jace. "You got your wife pregnant the first time you hooked up, but I don't think I got Cara pregnant."

"Whatever. It's how I snared Shelby, so I'm not sorry about it. There was no way she was looking for a relationship after losing her husband. The baby is what clarified some things."

"Again. Good for you. But the way I see it, it just kinda clicked into place, and I'm not a guy that does uncertainty. I care about her. So she needs to be in my life. Forever. Also, I can't have her hooking up with anybody else. Not gonna work. Not after that."

"Are you in love with her?" Chance asked.

The word scraped raw up against the inside of him.

"My feelings for her are stronger than my feelings for anyone else."

"No. That doesn't cut it. Are you in love with her? Are you giving her everything?"

"Everything I had to give," he said. "Look. I'm just not… I'm not into that. I'm not into this kind of impossible to define fantasy shit. I like what's tangible. That's why marriage is so fast. I don't just want to see where things go. I know I want her in my life forever. What more do I need to know?"

"I feel pretty damn strongly," said Chance, "that marriage is a lot about hope. And a whole lot about magic that you can't quite see or touch. Hell. Remember, I had to get amnesia to end up with my wife. Don't tell me there wasn't some kind of… Mystical intervention that happened there. It's not about just being practical. It's not about everything that you can see and touch. It's about something more than that."

He rebelled against that. "Not for me. I don't believe in that kind of thing."

"You better start. Otherwise… I think it's going to be tough for you."

"I've made the decision that I'm gonna make, and I've got everything that I want."

"Right now. But what can happen when she wants more from you."

"I don't know what more there could be. She's important to me. Essential enough that I'm willing to tie myself to her forever. I don't want to be with another woman. That became clear the minute that I touched her. I…"

"Why do you think this isn't love?" Kit asked.

"I don't know," he said. "Who cares what you call it. Maybe it is."

But something in him pushed back at that, and hard.

Like walls he had built around his soul were reinforcing themselves. Reminding him why they were there.

"I'm marrying her," he said. "What difference does it make what we call it?"

"I guess no difference,"

"There you go. Just say congratulations and that you're happy for me."

"I am," said Chance. "But the thing is, being with Juniper healed something inside of me. But you can't go into marriage the same and expect for it to work. Expect for it to heal you."

"I'm not looking to be healed," he said.

"Why not?" Kid asked.

"Because," he said. "Sophia is dead, and there's nothing anyone can do about it. She's gone. She'll always be gone. So the wound should never go away."

He looked down at the whiskey glass he was holding and frowned. It had a butterfly painted on the side.

He looked at the other glasses on the table in the room. Each had something different. It wasn't significant.

They didn't talk about him anymore after that. They just finished playing darts.

Thirteen

Cara felt so surrounded by love and warmth. Her future sisters-in-law fussed over her, and Jace's mother seemed to be just so happy.

And she felt partly like a fraud. She didn't know why. She and Jace were really getting married. They weren't making that up. It was just that… He hadn't said anything about being in love with her. And she couldn't figure out if she was being strange. If she was splitting hairs. Because Jace cared about her. She knew that. She would say it was indisputable even that he loved her. But she just had to wonder if his feelings had actually changed, or if they were just sleeping together.

And then she had to ask herself why it mattered. If it even did.

She had him in her life, the most stable relationship, and they were going to make it legal. So what did it matter what they called it.

Because you love him.

But what did that matter? Why would it be different if he said he loved her, or if he was in love?

She shoved all of her reservations to the side. And when Jace came back from playing darts with his brothers, he took her hand. "Want to drive over to my place?"

And she did. She really did. She wanted to spend the night with him. She wanted to solidify this whole thing. That their relationship had changed. And also that they were still them. Both felt so important right now. Both felt like it might be everything.

"You can follow me over."

She drove in her car behind him, down the bumpy dirt road that led away from the main house and toward the house he lived in on the property. She pulled up to his place, just behind him.

She got out and walked right to him. "Jace…"

She had been about to ask him where they might live when they were first married. If they would live here, if they would live at her place. But he wrapped his arm around her waist and pulled her to him. And pressed a kiss to her mouth. Fervent, hard and glorious. And maybe it wasn't the time to talk. Maybe it was okay for them to just feel for a while. Maybe it was just fine for them to retreat to this, because it felt right. Because it felt real. Because of all the crazy and uncertain things, this felt like a little bit of something. A little bit of certain. His kiss undid her.

And she wanted… She wanted to project everything that she felt right into him. Wished that she could be emitted to his chest. Wished that she could make him understand.

She wanted that more than anything. To show him. He had taken care of her for the first time, and the second time, he had given her confidence. The second time, he let her ride him, and it had been dirty and glorious and they'd been them. Even as they'd given each other pleasure.

But she wanted something else. Something more and deeper.

She wanted him to know. She wanted to show herself. The difference between love and being in love.

She wanted to see. If she could make it all for herself. If what she felt would be enough to sustain them. Would be enough to keep them together. He lifted her up off the ground, and she wrapped her arms around his neck, and she poured everything that she felt, everything that they were, into that kiss. All the relief that she had felt when he'd first been kind to her down by the creek all those years ago. The need she felt to fill that hole left behind by the sister that he loved so much. The years and years of friendship. Of telling each other things in confidence. Of being there for each other.

Her heart, her soul. Her gratitude for how he had

been there when her grandfather had died. For the way that he had effortlessly folded her into his family. And just the way she loved him. Her everything. Her heart.

She kissed him like she might die if she didn't, because she wasn't entirely certain that she wouldn't.

He walked them both back up the porch to his house and through the front door. But they didn't make it down the hall. They just barely made it to the couch. He laid her down on the soft surface, tearing at her clothes. They didn't talk. Didn't joke. Didn't laugh.

It was like a reckoning.

Everything was stripped away but their need. For each other. For this.

And already, she was so aroused by him. And already, she felt like she was lost in him. In this.

She clung to his shoulders and then realized she needed to get those clothes off of him. So she went from clinging to tearing, then her hands went to his belt buckle. Pushing the denim away from his body, as he wrenched her panties down her thighs, her sundress already somewhere on the floor.

His mouth was hungry, his hands demanding, and she loved it.

This man, this man who was desperate for her body—he wasn't a stranger anymore. This was part of them. Part of who they were now. And it was all the more powerful for it.

He put his hand between her thighs and teased her, tested her readiness.

"Now," she said, begging.

He settled himself between her legs and thrust home, establishing a wild rhythm that tested and tormented them both.

It was rough and hard, this coupling. And she loved it. She loved him.

She dug her fingers into the flesh of his shoulders, wrapped her legs around his waist. He said her name. Over and over again. Like a prayer or a curse, she didn't know, but she would take it all. Just as she would take all of him. And that was what he gave.

It was like a storm. The heat generated between them so bright and intense she thought she might be dying of it. And yet at the same time, it wasn't enough. She wondered if it would ever be enough.

She could feel him begin to tremble, shake. Could feel the edge of his control beginning to reach its end.

And when he found his release, it was on a growl and a shout, and she followed after him, squeezing him tight as he poured into her.

And then she kissed his mouth, his face. Said his name over and over again, because it was all she could think to say. Because he felt like the only thing. This moment felt like the only thing.

But then right at the same time, she looked to the future. To a bright, golden future shining with light, and butterflies. And she wanted that. Hoped for it. Reached for it.

And she knew—she knew that it was time. She knew that she had to say it.

"I love you, Jace."

He felt like he was dying. Really, like someone had ripped his lungs out. Like something in him had been broken, irrevocably. Irreparably.

I love you.

Of course she did. She was his best friend. He loved her too. It wasn't anything revolutionary. But it felt revolutionary, with him lying on top of her on the couch, still buried inside of her. Breathing hard. His mind flown from what had just passed between them, because it was more than pleasure. It always had been.

It was more than sex or release. More than orgasms.

It was something bigger. It was something that had changed them fundamentally. He had that feeling, when he'd seen her walking toward him tonight in that summer dress that he just stripped right off, he had that feeling.

He had this strange, crushing feeling all through the whole night. And he knew himself well enough to know it was when he wasn't acting with integrity. When he wasn't being honest about the things that were going on inside of himself. When his actions weren't matching up with what he knew to be important.

Yeah. That was when he felt these things. When he'd been hesitating to make his move in Lone Rock, to make his move with Cara. Not because he didn't know what to do, but because he hadn't wanted to do it.

And this was another reckoning. Like a gong going off inside of him.

And he didn't know why it felt so different. It was just that it did.

"That was amazing," he said.

And he wanted to cut his own tongue out.

"Yeah. But I said that I love you."

"I know," he said.

She drew away from him, but not all the way. She just sort of wiggled and scooted to the side. "Can you tell me about Sophia? A little bit more."

He nodded slowly. And it wasn't a weird change of subject. Not for him. Not for them.

"She loved butterflies," he said. "Everything had butterflies on it. The canopy on her bed, special hospital gown my parents bought her. Everything." He cleared his throat. "When I saw you that time…with your pink binder thing and it had those butterflies, I… It was like you were supposed to be there."

He heard himself. Heard himself saying all this stuff he wasn't supposed to believe. But he could remember that moment. Like he'd felt led to her. To this other girl who had butterflies.

It hurt to talk about it. It hurt to look back, because there was no good way to look forward. And he didn't like it. But the problem with putting down roots was it demanded a certain level of projecting. And maybe that was all part of the problem. Part of the shift. And maybe it was just that creating the heaviness in his chest.

"Little kids aren't supposed to get cancer," he said, his voice rough. "And a little boy isn't supposed to have to watch his sister die. A mother isn't supposed to have to watch her child die. Just not supposed to happen." And he knew there was no point to this. No point to raging against any of it. There never was. And so he never had. He had just turned everything off. Everything.

But now he felt like raging, for some reason. At what? There was nothing there.

But he wanted to do it all the same.

"She was the brightest, prettiest, most… She was just so fun. And being sick made it so she couldn't be fun. So she couldn't have fun. It wasn't fair. It's not fair. She was just a little girl that loved butterflies. How the hell is it right that she's gone?"

"It isn't. It's one of those big unfair things in the world."

"But how do you believe in miracles, in mysteries?

How do you dream and hope and all that shit that you do? How do you do it, Cara? Because I don't get it."

"Because I've accepted that there are things that I'll never know or understand. But I also don't believe that what happens to us here is the end. And so it's a deep tragedy within our understanding, but I just don't think that's where it stops. I can't believe that. Because I look around this world and I see miracles. I see miracles and shafts of sunlight and butterflies. There are always so many butterflies. Around you. Around me. I think she might be with you."

"No. I just… I can't…"

"I get it. It hurts to hope."

"Don't say that. Like you're patronizing me. Like I'm the one who's ridiculous. When you… You're the one that believes in all these things that you can't see."

"But there are so many things that we can't see, Jace. So many things. This, this between us. Don't you see the miracle in that? That you found me? But you found the girl with the pink butterfly Trapper Keeper. That you were there for me, like you were compelled to be. Don't you think there's something magic in that. And here we are, and we were each other's best friends all this time, all this time. And we can be more too. And isn't that a miracle. That not only are you my favorite person to talk to, but when we are together like this… It's so bright and hot and wonderful. What isn't miraculous about that?"

"And why couldn't I have the miracle that I wanted," he said, his words coming out hard. And he could see a brief flash of hurt in her eyes before she dismissed it.

"You know I didn't mean that," he said. "You know I didn't mean I didn't want you."

"I do," she said. "Because I know you. I know you don't want to hurt me. But I think I kind of get that you don't want to love me either."

Her words hit him in the center of his chest. They were quiet. And they weren't angry. They weren't accusing him of anything.

But they cut deep.

And they were true.

"What does that even mean? Between the two of us. What difference would it even make?"

She looked up at him, her eyes sad. "I don't know."

"Well until you know, what's the point of making it an issue?"

"That's fair. Let's go to bed."

"You still want to stay the night?"

"I still want to marry you."

And he would take that. Because he wanted to take care of her. He wanted to be with her. Like they had always been, and like this too. So even though he knew he messed up, he was going to go ahead and accept that.

"All right then. Let's go to bed."

"I just wanted to say... Or I need to make it clear."

She said nothing for a moment, and then she looked up at him, her green eyes firm and steely. "I don't need you."

She might as well have shot him directly in the chest. "What?"

"I don't need you. Even when I was a sad, flat-chested middle school girl, I didn't need you. I had been kicking along in my life just fine without you. You were great. You are great. But I would have survived if you weren't in my life."

She stood up then, naked and resolved, and he almost felt like he didn't have the right to look directly at her. "I'm tough. My mom is a drug addict who doesn't want me. Thankfully I don't remember very much from that time of my life. Very, very thankfully. Thankfully, mostly what I remember is my grandfather taking good care of me. I remember you being a good friend. And those things… They matter. But I don't need you. I didn't even need you for the hotel. I had it all worked out by myself, and I could've waited. I could've waited to remodel things and patch the raccoon hole. I could have."

"What exactly is your point?" he asked.

"My point is that I don't need you, Jace Carson. I just want you. So all of these things that you're doing, all of this stuff that you think makes you indispensable, that's not what it is. It's watching stupid movies with you. And it's spending the night in a hotel and fighting about ghosts. And about whether or not raccoons are cute or vicious. It's those little things that feel like the biggest things. The way that we talk about everything and talk about nothing. The fact that I did tell you that I hadn't been with anybody, even though I was drunk. And a little bit hitting on you. But no matter how that had worked out, I knew that I could trust you with that information. Because I've always known that. And that isn't about needing you, in the sense that I'm dependent on you. That is about wanting you around because you are the most trustworthy, wonderful, caring friend that anyone could've ever asked for. And that's not... It's not you needing to be my protector or my caregiver. That's you being you."

And he realized something, as those words came out of her mouth. She was right. She didn't need him. She was hands down the strongest, most incredible woman—person—that he knew. She had been through a lot, and she had a sense of humor and a firebrand personality. She was confident and capable. She had planned all her finances out in order to get the loan for the hotel in the first place, had even taken care of arranging all the logistics for the ghost sleepover.

She didn't need him.

He had told himself that she did for all these years.

But the truth of it was, he needed her.

He had told himself he had to protect her.

But it was himself he was protecting. All along.

And that was what every single movement that had happened since he had offered to spend the night with her at the hotel had been about. He had been looking for purchase, looking for roots, and of course, he had chosen to wrap them around her, because he didn't know what his life would look like without her.

She had become the thing that he leaned on.

He had fashioned her into a surrogate for every single thing that he missed. Everything he wanted and didn't have.

And he was… He couldn't give her what she wanted. He just couldn't do it.

Because he tried to think out that far ahead, and everything just went black. Because the idea of wanting anything, the idea of hoping for anything was something he was afraid to grab hold of.

"You should get dressed," he said, his voice scratchy.

"Why?"

"Because you should go home."

"This is going to be my home after we get married."

She was speaking with such a calm, firm voice, and he felt like an absolute dick for what he was about to say. But then, he felt that way about the entire situation. About everything. About the way that he had lied. To her. To himself. Because he had. He had found a way to convince himself that what he was doing was for her while he… Well he found a way to hold her close so that he could use her as a balm for his wound.

And at first it was all about taking care. Of somebody that he felt was vulnerable. Because he hadn't been able to take care of Sophia, had he? Not in a real way. Not in a meaningful way. She had died. So what had anything he'd done mattered? She had died, and that meant that he'd failed. And she just wasn't there. And there was a void where she should be. And he didn't know what he was, if he wasn't her older brother. Her friend.

And so he had become that for Cara, but that had gotten inconvenient when he'd started to become attracted to her, and for a while he'd been able to suppress it, because he was very, very good at suppressing emotion. Very good.

He had made a whole lifestyle out of it.

And that had worked for years, until she had looked him in the eye and told him that she was a virgin. And offered to let him be the one to change that. Yeah. It had all worked until that moment. And then... It had all gone to bright, burning hell. So he'd recast it. Recast her. Changing and shuffling the narrative into something, anything that allowed him to continue to run from the truth.

Because he really needed that. But she was there, calling him out, the way that she did. Because she was Cara Summers, and he was Jace Carson, and they were honest with each other.

To a point.

They had always lied about these things.

She had never told him that she wanted him, and he had never told her that he sometimes thought his life might fall apart if she wasn't in it.

Yeah, he went and traveled on the rodeo. He was away from her for large chunks of time sometimes, but she was always there. Waiting when he came back home. And it meant something. It mattered.

It was the reason he tried to live through those rides. That was just the truth of it. Knowing that she was there.

He had used her to give himself purpose.

He had used her as a conduit for all the spiritual things that he didn't allow himself to feel. Because she hoped enough for the both of them, was faithful enough for the both of them. Believed enough for the both of them. In the brightness and beauty of life, in a concept of miracles that he couldn't figure out how to hold in his hand, that she cradled in her palm effortlessly. The way she acted like her grandfather was simply a thought and a prayer away. The way she saw beauty in an old hotel, and potential in a half-empty Main Street.

What did he give to her, exactly?

And she said she loved him. And... And he was just broken.

But if he was going to do one thing, one good thing, it would be to stop this. To not continue to let his roots wrap around her, because all he would do is drag her down into the dirt, and she was meant for more than that.

She deserved more than that.

She hadn't chosen to be born to a mother that couldn't love her right. She hadn't chosen to have a father who wanted nothing to do with her. She didn't have to have a husband who was broken.

He'd wanted to keep her, because he was possessive. He wanted to keep her with him, to add security to his own life. And if he really wanted to do something for her, he needed to let her go. He needed to let her be free of him.

She only thought she was in love with him because of the sex. Because she had been a virgin. Because they'd been friends for so long.

"You should go home," he said again.

"Jace, you're scaring me."

"We can't get married, Cara. You want other things. Different things. Things I don't know how to give. And you're right. You're right. You don't need me. You stand on your own two feet just fine. I'm the one that's limping. I'm the one who's leaning on you. It's not right. I can't do it anymore, not now that I know."

"Jace, you idiot. Did it ever occur to you that I was fully aware of that?"

"What?"

"I know you. I know that there are things that are just really really tough."

"Why would you let me lean on you, if you don't need me?"

"I wouldn't fall onto the ground without you. How about that? But I have certainly leaned against you at many points over the years. You have been the single most important relationship in my life. Sorry, Grandpa. But it's been you, Jace. You taught me what I wanted from a friend. And then you taught me what to want from a lover. Those are huge things. But I've never been blind to the fact that you had cracks in your soul, Jace. Not ever. Because you went out of your way to befriend a sad, crying girl behind the middle school? Especially if he's cool and handsome and has all the friends he wants? You befriend the bird with the broken wing, because your wing is broken too. And neither of you can really fly. But together... We come pretty close."

"It's nice as a metaphor. But what it amounts to is me holding you down."

"I love you. What if I chose to be with you? What if I chose to be with you just because I wanted to be?"

"I'm telling you that I'm not going to be part of it. I'm not going to keep taking from you. Not when I can't give back."

"This is bullshit," she said. "You're just scared. You're scared, and you're too scared to admit that you're scared. I love you. I'm the one that admitted

it. I'm the one that took the step. And you can't because…" Her eyes filled with tears, and suddenly
she sucked in a sharp breath, like she had a realization in the moment between that last sentence and
this coming one. "And you just can't hope, can you?
You're afraid. You're afraid to hope that this could
become the best that it could be, because you think
it's easier to just imagine the worst. Or just imagine
nothing. Because you hoped that she would get well,
and she didn't."

He growled. "Forget it. Leave it alone."

"But that's it, isn't it? There is nothing that scares
you more in this world than hope. Because you've
hoped before. And it didn't go your way. It didn't go
anyone's way. It devastated you. It devastated you,
and you don't know what to do. Because you don't
trust that it wouldn't just happen again."

"Don't psychoanalyze me. You don't know what
it's like to have gone through what I have. You don't
have any idea what it's like. And maybe it's not psy-
chosis to refuse to believe in things that you can't
see. Maybe I'm not the one that's crazy."

"Well. Even if I'm wrong, at least I can think of
reasons to get out of bed in the morning. At night,
when I get under the covers, I think ahead. And that's
not a bad thing. I hope. Because what is life without
hope? It's what you have. You can't reach out and
take the love that is being offered to you, because
you can't look ahead. Because you're afraid to want

something that you can't…" She reached out and grabbed hold of him, placed her hands in his. "You want what you can hold in your hands. You're holding me. You're holding me. Can't you believe in me?"

No. He couldn't. Because he couldn't see the end of this. He couldn't see a way to fix this. Couldn't see a way to fix himself.

And he could not do that to her. He wouldn't.

"Go home."

And he did something he hadn't done in all the years since they'd met. He pulled away from her. He took a step back.

But she stood firm. She didn't get dressed like he'd ordered her to do. She didn't back away. She didn't even flinch. He could see deep anguish in her face, and he hated that he had put it there. But she didn't back down.

"All right. I will. But when you need somebody to talk to in the middle of the night, because everything is terrible, you call me. Because I'm your best friend. And you might be surprised to find out that I've been supporting you all these years, but I'm not."

"This changes things," he said. "I don't think that we can… I don't think that we can do this anymore."

"So wait a minute, you don't want to marry me, and you don't want to be my friend anymore?"

And that was when she faltered. When strong, beautiful Cara Summers looked like she might shatter. And he really stood there and marinated in his own sense of fear and anguish, because it had been a long time since he had felt anything like this. He thought that he was going to break. And he hadn't thought that there was any fragile thing left inside of him.

"I can't be. Because it would just be me hanging on to you when you need to be let go. It would be me keeping you in a place where you hope that something can be different when it can't be. You can't love me. Not anymore."

"You don't get to tell me what to do."

"I'm right. I'm just… I'm right about this, Cara."

"You're leaving me with nothing," she said, her voice frayed, wretched. "You're leaving me with nobody. You have your whole family, and what are you leaving me with?"

"Cara…"

"No. No. You don't get to do this. You don't get to try to make me feel bad for you. Or make me think that you're doing the right thing, that you're being all brave and self-sacrificing by doing this. You're just being a coward. You're ruining us. You are ruining the life that we could have. Because you're scared. And I will not let you turn it into anything else. I know you too well for that. That's the problem with breaking up with your best friend, Jace. I just see through it. Even if you can't." And then she did pick up her clothes. And she dressed, and she walked out of the house without a backward glance, and he felt like she had taken the entire world with her.

Butterflies and all.

Fourteen

She should have gone straight back to her house, but she didn't. Instead, she went to the hotel. She went to the hotel, because it just seemed like maybe it would be a little bit more comforting than being by herself. Though, she didn't think that anything could comfort her at this point.

As soon as she walked in, she was comforted by something. Maybe the presence of the raccoon. Maybe the presence of the orb. She didn't know. Or maybe it was just that… She could lie to herself here. She could remember when they had been here last, and they had been full of dreams, and he had stood there and asked her to marry him.

Like they could have a future. A future that looked so different than one she had ever imagined for herself. A future that looked bigger, brighter and better.

She had always been alone. She had always been the one that people just didn't love enough. And she knew that wasn't fair. Not to herself. She knew it wasn't fair to blame herself for this, not when Jace's fears about love were about him. They weren't about her. But it didn't mean they didn't brush up against all the tender places inside of her. That it didn't feel jagged and wrong. That it didn't make her feel lost and sad and all of fourteen years old again and somehow just not good enough. Just not enough.

Because if she was enough, couldn't she make him… Change?

Couldn't she make him see?

Couldn't she make him let go.

He doesn't want to let go. And if he doesn't want to let go, nothing can make him. Nobody can make him.

She knew that was true. Logically, she knew it was true. But nothing was logical about heartbreak.

She paused at the bottom of the stairs. Jace had broken her heart. She was literally living in her worst nightmare. She had fallen in love with him, and he had rejected her. And he hadn't just broken up with her… He had ended their friendship.

Of all the things she had ever worried about, she had never worried about that one thing. She had thought that it would be torture to be with him, and then have to watch him move on with other women, all the while at his side as his faithful companion.

She had never imagined that he would end the friendship completely.

She stood there. Waiting to fall to pieces. Waiting to fall apart.

And she didn't see any glowing lights, but suddenly, she felt one. At the center of her chest, glowing within her soul. She waited to feel isolated, because Jace had been the only person that she'd ever had in her life long-term. The only one who was still here.

But she didn't feel alone. Because her grandfather was with her. And maybe something else was too. Someone else.

Because whatever he thought, whatever he said, love didn't end when someone died, and neither did they. Everything that they were to you was still there. And all the love that they had ever given you, and that you had ever given in return.

She knew that. It was why she was standing in this hotel. It was why she was here at all.

Her grandfather being gone didn't erase the love that he'd given her.

And Jace ending things didn't undo everything that they been.

She put her hand on her chest, and she felt like she might have a broken heart, but even within that... Even within it... She felt a rush of gratitude.

Because he couldn't undo all these years.

He couldn't take the love that he'd given her already and cut it out of her heart, take it out of her soul. Because it was part of her. Woven into the very fabric of who she was.

This was like a death.

But like death… It wasn't really the end.

Because she loved him. And she had all the years before. She would have all the years after too. And she wished… She wished that it would look different. But it was the same as loving people who were gone, she supposed. She wished that it could look different too. But it couldn't. And yes, it was much more within his control to make this something that was happy instead of sad and painful, but… But it simply was. It simply was what it was.

It was painful. But there was beauty in it too, and he couldn't take the beauty away.

It was part of who she was. And what she had to trust was that it was part of who he was too.

Enough that it would never really go away. Enough that he would never really be able to be rid of her.

Of course, that cut both ways. And she would never be able to get rid of him either.

But she didn't want to.

Even if it hurt, she didn't want to. And that was the difference between the woman she was now, and the girl that he had found crying by the creek. She had needed to be different. She had wanted to escape. Had wanted to fight and run away.

And the woman she was now didn't want to do

any of those things. She was ready to stand firm and tall. He had said that he had tried to grow his roots around her, and he had dragged her down. But the reality was, her own roots went deep. She knew who she was. And it would take more than a storm to knock her over.

She knew who she was.

She was a woman who loved a man who wouldn't love her back.

And it hurt.

But she wouldn't falter or dissolve, or hide from the pain in drugs and in other meaningless relationships the way that her mother had done. Or just… Simply not show up the way her father had done.

And she wouldn't let it steal her hope, the way grief and pain had done to Jace.

And it wasn't because she was better. It was simply because… She had been given enough love in her life, that it sustained her now.

She walked up the stairs to the bedroom that she had shared with Jace. And she wasn't afraid of it. Wasn't afraid of seeing anything potentially spooky. Because there was nothing scary about it. She couldn't see the future. But there was nothing scary about that either.

Because she could believe that there would be something better.

She had to.

She had to.

* * *

Well he'd done it. He'd broken everything. He'd broken the world. Utterly and irrevocably. It was like he had reached up and hammered a nail into the sky and let it all shatter. Then it all rained down on him.

And that was more fanciful thinking than he ever allowed himself. Because he never allowed himself to... To hope.

She was right about that.

The other thing he had never allowed himself to truly believe was that he had the potential to be hurt more than he already had been. He thought that he had a clear-eyed view of life. And here he was, standing in the middle of a screwed up situation that he had created, feeling like he would never sort out the wreckage. Feeling like he would never be able to stand up straight again.

What had he done?

He had lost his sister. She had been the single most important person in his life. His best friend. And he had met Cara, and being with her, being near her had done something to finally soothe the ache inside of him. And now... He'd sent her away. He'd chosen to not have her. And he had...

It was him. It was his fault. He ruined it. He couldn't stand to sit here for another minute. He didn't sit. It wasn't the thing that he did. He was decisive.

And look where it got you.

He didn't look ahead because all he could see was blackness. Bleakness. Blank despair.

He walked out of the house, and he started to walk down the trail that went behind the place. The moon was full, so he could see just enough to walk without tripping over anything. The trail wound up the side of the mountain, through a thick copse of trees, where it all went pitch-black.

And this… This seemed right. It seemed fair. It seemed like a look at his life. A look at his future.

But he pressed on through, and when he came to the top of the mountain, he looked up and there were stars. Because, impossibly, the world was still turning, and everything was still up in the sky, and he hadn't shattered it at all. It just felt that way. Because it was him. Because it was his heart.

Dammit all.

And no matter how hard he had tried to make sure that it didn't… That it didn't want anything, not ever again… No matter how hard he tried, she had gotten in there. She was under his skin. She was in him, no matter how hard he had tried.

He sat down, right there on the mountainside, and looked out at the broad expanse of everything.

"She thinks that you're out there, Sophia," he said, feeling like an idiot. But he had nothing. He had nothing to hope for, nothing to lose, nothing to gain. He might as well sit there and talk to the night sky. "But I just can't feel anything. Or I'm afraid to. I wanted to believe that there was nothing left to hope for so that I could never get hurt again, and here I am. I haven't hurt this bad since… Not since you. But I did it to myself. I did it to the person that I care about most in this world." He felt a stabbing sensation in his chest. "I love her. I am in love with her, and I sent her away, because I'm too afraid to claim that. Because I'm too afraid to want it."

He closed his eyes, and he waited for something. For inspiration to strike, a lightning bolt from heaven.

Yeah. Because you could ignore all that and say you didn't believe in it, and then just get a sign the minute that you asked.

It was dark, and so was his soul.

He lowered his head, keeping his eyes closed, and he waited. He waited there all night. Until the sun started to rise up over the view in front of him. And it was the strangest thing. Just as the golden rays of light began to touch the brush on the rocks all around him, the flowers, he saw them. Hundreds of them. Little white butterflies, rising up from every surface. All around.

And he felt…

Love. Like he never imagined before, like he never felt it before. Like everyone who had ever stood in the spot before him was still there, like Sophia wasn't gone.

"You tried to tell me," he said, looking all around. "But I'm a particular kind of dumbass, so you can't just send a few. I guess I needed a whole butterfly storm."

And he could see it, like he was looking straight past that horizon. A life and the world all lit up with this kind of love. And he could see himself with Cara.

His Cara.

And once he could see that... Once he could believe it... In this thing that had felt intangible and impossible only a few hours before, he knew.

That he loved her.

And that life might not come with guarantees or certainty. That the world was a harsh and dangerous place.

But love was what made it worthwhile. Love was what endured.

Love didn't work all by itself. You needed faith to go along with it.

And that's what he'd been missing. The ability to believe, in this thing that was bigger than he was.

In this thing he couldn't control. It had been easier to do when she was beside him. Bright and perfect. But maybe he needed this moment, to try and see the light without taking hers.

Because he needed to bring back what he was taking. Needed to give equal to what he was getting.

And he was ready now.

He could only hope that she would still want him after how badly he had messed up.

But he'd loved her for a very long time. He could

see that now. When he looked back and forward, and at the present moment, it all added up to love.

Maybe that was why he so obsessively didn't like to look at his life.

He'd been living a whole life.

But he was done lying. And he was done running.

Unless it was straight to her.

Fifteen

When she woke up the next morning and heard pounding downstairs, she was afraid that it was a raccoon. Or maybe a ghost.

She got out of bed, and when she moved the curtain, it disturbed a little white butterfly. She paused for a moment and looked at it, watched it flutter around the room, before the knocking became more insistent. And then she ran down the stairs, and she could see him through the window.

Jace.

She flung the door open. "How did you know that I would be here?"

"Well, it's not the first place I've been."

"It's really early," she said.

He took a step inside, and her heart began to throb painfully. "No. It's really late, actually."

"It's sunrise," she said.

"I just mean... I'm late with this. Everything I said last night was me running scared. But you knew that already. And I was... I was wrong. Everything I did to you was wrong. Everything I said to you was wrong. And everything you said to me was true. I was scared. More than scared, I've been paralyzed. When Sophia died, it was like my ability to hope that things would turn out okay was just... Killed along with her. But it's a bad tribute, if nothing else. I'm here. And I'm alive, and I've been acting like a part of me died. Except I had you. And you were that bright spot. And you know what, I didn't have to know very much as long as you were with me. It was only when I was forced to sit in the darkness of what my life looked like without you that I had to try and find the light for myself. That I had to try and see past the horizon line. And I can't see a future without you."

She sucked in a hard breath, and she waited.

"Because I love you," he said.

"Thank God."

"Yeah." She wrapped her arms around his neck and she just hugged him. Held him for a long moment. "I really love you too."

"Still? Even after... After everything?"

"Maybe especially after everything. Because this was a lot of work. I know it was. Because I know you."

"I have to tell you. I wanted a sign. Something.

And you know that I was desperate if I was asking for signs. And this morning… There were all these white butterflies, everywhere. And I can't explain it."

She pulled back and looked at him, and she laughed. "I saw one this morning too."

"Cara Summers," he said, his voice rough. "I can't believe that I'm about to say this. But I think that this is meant to be."

Epilogue

They didn't end up rushing down the aisle. They took their time. Because Jace wasn't afraid, and he didn't need all those external things to prove to him that what they had wasn't going to evaporate, and because Cara decided that she wanted to get married at the hotel, so she wanted it finished before the event.

They'd gotten married in the newly landscaped backyard, and had the reception both inside and outside.

The old restaurant and bar in the far wing of the hotel was beautifully renovated, and it was set up with free drinks for all of their guests.

And just behind the bar, on that top shelf, was Grandpa's whiskey bottle.

Late in the evening, when the guests were all leaving, and it was Jace and Cara, sitting in the bar, her in her wedding dress, and him in his tux, she lifted a glass of whiskey up toward the bottle. "To Grandpa," she said.

"To Mitch," Jace agreed. "Thanks, old man. For everything."

She smiled. "You're even talking to him now."

"It just doesn't feel half so strange. Not anymore."

"Why do you think that is? Is it just because of the butterflies?"

He shook his head. "No. It's because of the love. Because that is a miracle, Cara, it really is. And once you believe in one miracle, it's not so hard to start believing in all of them."

She smiled. "I love you, Jace. You're my best friend."

"I love you too. And you know, you're definitely my best friend, but even better… You're my wife."

"I like that, husband."

"I think it's time to go upstairs," he said, tipping his glass back.

"You have a one-track mind."

"Yeah. I do. But you know what… After… After what I really want to do is dream about the future."

"I didn't think you did dreams."

"That was before."

"Before what?"

"Before you made my life the best dream of all."

* * * * *

COMING NEXT MONTH FROM

⊕HARLEQUIN

DESIRE

#2929 DESIGNS ON A RANCHER

Texas Cattleman's Club: The Wedding • by LaQuette

When big-city designer Keely Tucker is stranded with Jacob Chatman, the sexiest, most ambitious rancher in Texas, unbridled passion ignites. But will her own Hollywood career dreams be left in the rubble?

#2930 BREAKAWAY COWBOY

High Country Hawkes • by Barbara Dunlop

Rodeo cowboy Dallas Hawkes has an injured shoulder and a suspicious nature. Giving heartbroken Sierra Armstrong refuge at his ranch is a nonstarter. But the massage therapist's touch can help heal his damaged body. And open a world of burning desire in his lonely bed...

#2931 FRIENDS...WITH CONSEQUECES

Business and Babies • by Jules Bennett

The not-so-innocent night CEO Zane Westbrook spent with his brother's best friend, Nora Monroe, was supposed to remain a secret. But their temporary fling turns permanent when she reveals she's expecting Zane's baby!

#2932 AFTER THE LIGHTS GO DOWN

by Donna Hill

It's lights, camera, *scandal* when competing morning-show news anchors Layne Davis and Paul Waverly set their sights on their next career goals. Especially as their ambitions and attraction collide on set...and seductive sparks explode behind closed doors!

#2933 ONE NIGHT WAGER

The Gilbert Curse • by Katherine Garbera

When feisty small-town Indy Belmont takes on bad boy celebrity chef Conrad Gilbert in a local cook-off, neither expects a red-hot attraction. Winning his strong, sexy arms may be prize enough! But only if Indy can tame her headstrong beast...

#2934 BIG EASY SECRET

Bad Billionaires • by Kira Sinclair

Jameson Neally and Kinley Sullivan are two of the best computer hackers in the world. Cracking code is easy. But cracking the walls around their guarded hearts? Impossible! When the two team up on a steamy game of cat and mouse, will they catch their culprit...or each other?

YOU CAN FIND MORE INFORMATION ON UPCOMING HARLEQUIN TITLES, FREE EXCERPTS AND MORE AT HARLEQUIN.COM.

HDCNM0123

Get 4 FREE REWARDS!

We'll send you 2 FREE Books plus 2 FREE Mystery Gifts.

FREE Value Over $20

Both the **Harlequin® Desire** and **Harlequin Presents®** series feature compelling novels filled with passion, sensuality and intriguing scandals.

YES! Please send me 2 FREE novels from the Harlequin Desire or Harlequin Presents series and my 2 FREE gifts (gifts are worth about $10 retail). After receiving them, if I don't wish to receive any more books, I can return the shipping statement marked "cancel." If I don't cancel, I will receive 6 brand-new Harlequin Presents Larger-Print books every month and be billed just $6.30 each in the U.S. or $6.49 each in Canada, a savings of at least 10% off the cover price, or 6 Harlequin Desire books every month and be billed just $5.05 each in the U.S. or $5.74 each in Canada, a savings of at least 12% off the cover price. It's quite a bargain! Shipping and handling is just 50¢ per book in the U.S. and $1.25 per book in Canada.* I understand that accepting the 2 free books and gifts places me under no obligation to buy anything. I can always return a shipment and cancel at any time by calling the number below. The free books and gifts are mine to keep no matter what I decide.

Choose one: ☐ **Harlequin Desire**
(225/326 HDN GRJ7)

☐ **Harlequin Presents Larger-Print**
(176/376 HDN GRJ7)

Name (please print)

Address   Apt. #

City   State/Province   Zip/Postal Code

Email: Please check this box ☐ if you would like to receive newsletters and promotional emails from Harlequin Enterprises ULC and its affiliates. You can unsubscribe anytime.

Mail to the Harlequin Reader Service:
IN U.S.A.: P.O. Box 1341, Buffalo, NY 14240-8531
IN CANADA: P.O. Box 603, Fort Erie, Ontario L2A 5X3

Want to try 2 free books from another series! Call 1-800-873-8635 or visit www.ReaderService.com.

*Terms and prices subject to change without notice. Prices do not include sales taxes, which will be charged (if applicable) based on your state or country of residence. Canadian residents will be charged applicable taxes. Offer not valid in Quebec. This offer is limited to one order per household. Books received may not be as shown. Not valid for current subscribers to the Harlequin Presents or Harlequin Desire series. All orders subject to approval. Credit or debit balances in a customer's account(s) may be offset by any other outstanding balance owed by or to the customer. Please allow 4 to 6 weeks for delivery. Offer available while quantities last.

Your Privacy—Your information is being collected by Harlequin Enterprises ULC, operating as Harlequin Reader Service. For a complete summary of the information we collect, how we use this information and to whom it is disclosed, please visit our privacy notice located at corporate.harlequin.com/privacy-notice. From time to time we may also exchange your personal information with reputable third parties. If you wish to opt out of this sharing of your personal information, please visit readerservice.com/consumerschoice or call 1-800-873-8635. **Notice to California Residents**—Under California law, you have specific rights to control and access your data. For more information on these rights and how to exercise them, visit corporate.harlequin.com/california-privacy.

HDHP22R3

HARLEQUIN
PLUS

Announcing a **BRAND-NEW** multimedia subscription service for romance fans like you!

Read, Watch and Play.

Experience the easiest way to get the romance content you crave.

Start your **FREE 7 DAY TRIAL** at
<u>www.harlequinplus.com/freetrial</u>.

HARPLUS0822